THE JOURNEY OF KAROLINE OLSEN

THE JOURNEY OF KAROLINE OLSEN

ANN HANIGAN KOTZ

BookPress®

publishing

This is a work of fiction. Names, characters, businesses, places, events, locales, and incidents are either the products of the author's imagination or used in a fictitious manner. Any resemblance to actual persons, living or dead, or actual events is purely coincidental.

Published in Des Moines, Iowa, by:
Bookpress Publishing
P.O. Box 71532
Des Moines, IA 50325
www.BookpressPublishing.com

Publisher's Cataloging-in-Publication Data

Names: Kotz, Ann Hanigan, author.
Title: The Journey of Karoline Olsen / Ann Hanigan Kotz.
Description: Des Moines, IA: Bookpress Publishing, 2023.
Identifiers: LCCN: 2022914944 | ISBN 978-1-947305-51-9
Subjects: LCSH Norwegian Americans--Fiction. | Pioneers--Fiction. | Frontier and pioneer life--Fiction. | Women--Fiction. | Middle West--History--19th century--Fiction. | Historical fiction.| BISAC FICTION / Historical / General
Classification: LCC PS3611.O74938 J68 2023 | DDC 813.6--dc23

First Edition
Printed in the United States of America
10 9 8 7 6 5 4 3 2 1

For my mother, Evonne.
Thank you for sharing your stories.

1905

Perched up on the seat, Karoline peered down into the wagon. A fresh layer of golden straw, clean and smelling of the barn, covered the entire bed. Karoline didn't want to think about what lay below the straw. Underneath were large, twenty-five-pound blocks of ice cut from the Cedar River in the winter and stored in the Cedar Falls Icehouse. The workmen had carried the blocks with ice tongs, their muscles bulging with the weight of each. The frozen blocks were packed around the body, which was wrapped in a heavy canvas tarp to keep it from deteriorating until she could put him into the ground. Karoline had traveled more than two weeks to make the trip from Soldier to Cedar Falls to retrieve him. Now, she needed make the journey home.

She thought back to the stifling morning her son-in-law had made the trip from town to bring her the telegram. She was working in the garden, harvesting tomatoes and pulling weeds. His words,

"Kristoffer is dead," ripped her roots out of the ground. Kristoffer, her husband, had been where she had planted her life for twenty-two years. Those shocking words traveled through her body and made each part of her numb. She felt like she was releasing her inner self, the person she was. It leaked out of her and pooled on the ground around her. She felt flat and empty. Once her brain began to process thoughts again, her always-practical self inwardly asked, how am I going to get him home?

Kristoffer had been in northern Iowa, working on a farm to bring in extra money for the family. This was not the first time he had left to work for someone else. Farming was a precarious occupation that often brought more worry and sorrow than bounty. The current drought in western Iowa had pushed him north to look for farm work, and he had written Karoline two weeks ago to tell her that he had found a position as a general farm hand—milking cattle, harvesting alfalfa, and slopping hogs—and had sent the address along with it. It was only ten miles or so north of Cedar Falls.

When Karoline finally arrived in Cedar Falls, she was informed that, while out in the field cutting hay, his appendix had burst. The country doctor possessed no means to operate. Even with a competent surgeon, the chances of survival were unlikely. Kristoffer, lying on a bed in a stranger's house, had languished for five days, the infection spreading throughout his body, until it killed him. The farm family had been kind enough to bring him to Cedar Falls so he could be embalmed and packed in ice to await her arrival.

The solo trip across the state had not been easy. With no direct route, she had often been forced to take side roads, requiring her to stop frequently to ask for directions. Not surprisingly, people showed kindness. Once they discovered her purpose, they offered her food and lodging. One Norwegian family offered to send their oldest boy with her, but she declined. She needed to make this trip alone. Iowa, their third home after Norway and then Minnesota, was like an older brother to them: lots of advice from neighbors and a helping hand any time they reached out, and even sometimes when they didn't. Now, to make it back to Soldier, she would most likely need that brotherly help again.

Making her way home, carrying her husband's body, Karoline had nothing but time to think about her husband, her marriage, her life. The last time she had seen him, just as he was walking away from her to start his trip, he had broken her heart for the final time. There had been no words since then. And there would never be words again.

Karoline, staring into the wagon, knew that her heavy task might be her breaking point. She came to this country as a naïve bride, relying heavily on Kristoffer; now she was a more seasoned woman, having learned to rely on herself. Being alone in this current task brought a familiar feeling that she knew well. This feeling, one of determination and self-reliance, had evolved over her life as Kristoffer's wife. Karoline knew she was going to need these abilities to get her through the final trial.

After the men had affixed the tarp to the wagon bed, Karoline clucked her tongue to her horses and began the longest journey of her life.

1882

Karoline traveled with her family—her father, Gulbran Evensen; her mother, Armaliea; her sister, Sophie; and her youngest brother, Rikhard—through the hills of Norway to attend the annual Christmas celebration at the Lutheran church. The entire Lutheran community of Kristiania would attend. The Christmas dance was the biggest celebration of the year, and Karoline had eagerly counted the days until its arrival. She loved to see everyone's best clothing and to be in the midst of happy greetings and loud laughter. It made her feel warm. The celebrants danced, ate homemade food, played games, and shared the holiday cheer and local gossip. As usual, her father, a well-known violinist in the congregation, would be part of the band. Because her family had traveled eight miles in deep snow, they would be staying with their mother's sister Anja and her husband Daniel until the day after Christmas.

Their family was one of the last to arrive, and Karoline, straining on her tiptoes, looked through the crowd to find her best friend, Runa Hansen. The rustic hall, normally cold and empty and stark, had been transformed for the festivity. Some of the women from church had placed candles along the long tables dotted around the perimeter of the hall, which brought a cozy and somewhat romantic feel. Other tables hosted red table runners, brought from home by some of the women, and boughs of pine lying down the centers, filling the building with fresh outdoor scent. Hundreds of congregants in brightly colored clothes were dancing on the floor, sitting along the side, standing in groups chatting about the latest news. The room was warm with the heat of people.

Karoline finally spied her friend standing among a group of other girls. Karoline joined them and watched the young couples dancing on the floor. The gaggle of young women gossiped about each couple as well as each single girl sitting along the side of the room. Karoline was excited to someday be one of those young couples with a fellow of her own.

After watching a few dances, the two friends split off from the group. Karoline and Runa were like sisters though Runa was tall and blonde while Karoline was petite with thick auburn hair and dark blue eyes. Tonight, she had it plaited and wound around her head like an angel with a halo. The color of her hair and eyes contrasted with her fair skin. She had always wished that she had blonde hair like Runa, but red ran in her father's family, making it impossible that she would ever be blonde. Both now seventeen, they had experienced common travails and celebrations. Their relationship had started when they were young girls. They met at a church picnic when they were seven. After that, they were fast friends, spending summer days at the Evensens' pond and winter weekend nights tucked together in Runa's bed on a sleepover. Karoline shared all of her secrets and sorrows with Runa, who was a good listener and helped Karoline reason through any of her troubles. As they had aged, they had dreamed of their weddings and children. They thought that they would one day live close to each other and raise their children together.

Now, they considered themselves close to the marrying age and stood on the side of the dance floor, speculating who among the crowd of young men might soon one day become a husband. They had played this game often as young girls. As young women, they treated it as serious business. Runa had her eye on Valter Olsen, a tall young man of twenty-eight. Her father would be pleased with the match considering he was the oldest in the family of eleven children, so he would be the only one to inherit a portion of the farm.

His brothers would either become farm hands for someone else, join the military, or work in the logging industry. Until then, the boys helped their father farm. His sisters would hopefully marry men who would inherit as well. Until then, when the girls turned twelve, they were sent to work on neighboring farms to complete chores, help raise the children, and essentially make life easier for a mother with so many small faces to think of. Karoline had not been sent to toil in someone else's house because their family was small, and her father felt that it was beneath them to collect from their children's labors. However, Runa's family had labored her to a family in town as a nanny to their three young children.

Runa had caught Valter's eye and was now out on the dance floor with him. Karoline, too shy to show herself around to the young men, had taken a seat with the older ladies on the perimeter. Out of the group of men, walking toward them, came Kristoffer Olsen, Valter's younger brother. He was a handsome man with thick, dark, wavy hair; ruddy skin; and bright blue eyes. His face was framed by a beard and mustache that matched his hair. It was well groomed and added a softness to his high, sharp cheekbones. Kristoffer was twenty-seven, ten years her senior. He spied Karoline from the other side of the room and walked toward her. Karoline looked around her, hoping that he intended to ask another young woman, but she was the only available one in the group.

"Miss Evensen, I would be very pleased if you would dance with me."

"I would, but my father asked me to make sure that he had a glass of water near him. I have neglected my duty and must go get him the water," she lied.

"Maybe the next dance, then?"

"Perhaps," she said, looking around for a gracious way to escape.

Truthfully, she was shy around anyone but family and couldn't think of any conversation topics, and the waltz put her too close to him to be silent. So that she didn't look like a liar, she got up and retrieved a glass of water for her father, who had been playing with the band for over an hour. When she set the glass down on a stool near him, he looked at her with a small smile and then looked toward Kristoffer. From his place on the band platform, he had seen her decline him. He knew his daughter well and understood her delivery of the water.

Karoline reasoned that going back to her seat would only invite other young men to ask her to dance. She decided to volunteer her help at the dessert tables. The tables were decked with the women's finest baking: caramel pear galettes, boiled Christmas fruit cakes, chocolate cakes, bread pudding with a whiskey sauce, several pecan pies, and several batches of krumkakes. She and her mother had baked one of those batches. Because of the special event, they had included orange and cardamom in the batter. It was Karoline's job to cook the batter on the iron and then roll the flat pieces into cones while they were still hot. The Evensen women had wanted to make the desserts special, so they decided to fill them with whipped cream, which was infused with cinnamon. To keep the filling from melting, they had left it out of the cones and kept it outside in the cold. When they arrived at the church, her mother had quickly filled the golden shells. Among all of the desserts, theirs were being consumed the fastest.

Karoline stood behind the tables as if her job was to serve the desserts to the guests. She thought that it made her look purposeful, so much so that any of the young men would leave her alone to do her job. Just as she was starting to feel relaxed again as she watched the dancers, Kristoffer walked toward the dessert table.

He said, "I see you have many jobs to do tonight. I was hoping that I could get at least one dance with you."

"Oh, *ja*," she said. "I don't know. I have to make sure that I take care of the dessert tables. I think my parents would be disappointed if I neglected to do my duty."

"I see. No one more than I can appreciate a job being done well. But I asked your father for permission to dance with you. He said it was completely your decision, but he did not mind. So, Karoline, please dance with me?"

Embarrassed that she had been caught, Karoline's cheeks flushed red, and having no more excuses to decline, she replied, "I would be pleased."

He brought her out on the Halling dance. She completed her own small twirls and clapped while completing a large circle around him as he danced in circles and artfully executed complicated foot maneuvers and kicks. To her delight and surprise, Kristoffer was such an attractive and skilled dancer that the other dancers made a circle around the outside of the dance floor and clapped while he and she became the show. His long frame and dark hair gave him an elegant look. His bright blue eyes shone with joy as he showed off his agility. She was glad that the male dancer, like a brightly plumed bird, was the main attraction and only brought her into his dance at certain points. She didn't need nearly the skill that Kristoffer needed to complete the dance. At the end, though, both of their faces were bright red and glistening from their exertion. Kristoffer took her hand and invited her to stand outside with him to cool off. Her shyness had transformed to admiration, and she wanted to ask him about his dancing.

When they stepped outside the door, she asked, "How did you learn such skill? I've never seen anyone who could jump so high and make such complicated foot movements."

"My mother," he said. "She taught me at a young age. I was the only one of us boys who enjoyed dancing, so she has been my partner for many years."

Cooled by the night air, they decided to return to the celebration. The conversation then turned from his dancing to his working as a laborer. When he turned sixteen, he went to work for the Nilsens. He now worked in the logging camps and had been saving money for his future.

"What do you plan to do?" she asked.

"I would like to own my own farm," he replied. He could see the quizzical look on her face. In Norway, each family split their farm with the first son. At any given time, there could be three to four families living on the same plot of land, trying to feed many mouths. Many of the farms were in debt, so even if a young man was a first son, there might not be enough income to support a family. Since he was the second son, there was no inherited land for him. Additionally, there was really no land to buy.

"How do you plan to buy a farm?" she questioned.

"Yes," he said. "I can understand your skepticism." I am going to buy a farm in America and raise my family there. My cousin has already crossed and found fertile land to purchase. He wrote to my family about it. It's the only way someone like myself can become his own man."

Karoline was shocked at his lofty aspirations but also a little pleased that he wanted to work his own land instead of working for someone else.

"When do you plan to go to America?"

"In another year. I have money for my ship passage, but I need to finish saving for my wife's passage."

Karoline physically blanched, which he noticed. She could see the small glint in his eye and read the slight smirk on his face

"Are you playing me for a fool?" She knew that young men liked to play pranks on each other. She was certain she had fallen into such a prank and felt embarrassed that she had been so gullible.

"No, I'm so sorry. I meant for the wife I plan to marry before I leave Norway. I want to make sure that I marry someone who comes from the same place, speaks the same language, and can share common memories with me."

"So you don't have a wife right now? A fiancé?" At that point, Karoline realized she might have been dancing with someone else's man, which meant she would become the subject of gossip.

"Not as of today," he said. "But, I think I'll know the right girl when I meet her."

Kristoffer courted Karoline several times over the next three months. During those courtings, they spent time with Karoline's family—playing games; listening to her father play the violin; and taking short walks, her sister serving as a chaperone.

Their conversation was easy, and they shared the same goals: they both wanted a family with many children, and neither wanted to work for someone else for the rest of their lives.

She felt certain he was the right man to marry and hoped he felt the same about her. She was growing quite fond of Kristoffer, but she did not love him. Karoline felt somewhat torn about her future plans. Her vision of marriage included strong, passionate love. She thought they would love each other so much that they couldn't stand to be even a day apart. Her mother had told her that first a woman must find the right partner; then, she will grow to love him. Armaliea explained that having the same values and respect for one another was more important than love. Love could be grown. But if you did not respect your spouse or the couple did not share the same values, the marriage would never work.

While she and Kristoffer courted, Karoline had neglected her friendship with Runa. On a Sunday afternoon, Runa's only free day, the young women met at Evensen Pond for a picnic. Runa wanted all of the specifics when Karoline told her the exciting news of her growing relationship. Karoline shared details of their dates, pieces of their conversation, and her mother's advice about love and marriage. When Karoline included the part about moving to America, Runa's eyes betrayed her disappointment.

"I always thought that we would live next door to each other and raise our children together," she said.

"Me too," Karoline replied. "Maybe you will marry a man, and he will move to America as well. Maybe you'll marry Valter Olsen."

"I don't think so. I haven't seen him since the dance. And besides, as a first son, he'll live here on their farm."

"We'll stay in touch. We've been friends since childhood. Nothing will keep us apart," Karoline promised.

After four months of courting, Kristoffer sat with her parents in their kitchen and firmly asked for the privilege of marrying her. "I wish to marry your daughter," he said firmly. "I care deeply for her and respect her. I promise that I will take care of her always and give her the best life that I can. I am asking for your consent."

They gave their consent; however, they were reluctant when he

told them he planned to take her to America. Knowing the time and
expense it took to travel that distance, Gulbran and Armaliea had dif-
ficulty coming to terms with potentially never seeing their daughter
again. There might never be family dinners with her, Kristoffer, and
their children. They might never set eyes on their own grandchildren.
If tragedy struck, they were too far away to comfort Karoline or help
her. Armaliea was silently hoping that Kristoffer would not have the
money to leave Norway. Gulbran, being a first son, understood the
fate of the other sons. He had always said that he had been kissed by
the stars because he was born first. He understood that the couple
would always live in a rented house and would work someone else's
land. Their own children would follow the same path, and he loved
his daughter enough to want better for her and her future children.
America offered land for all of them. It was the single best solution
to a better life.

1905

As Karoline rode along with Kristoffer's body, she watched her matching bays make their way in synchronization. They reminded her of a perfect, married couple—very different from herself and Kristoffer. The horses, nearly the same ones Kristoffer had owned as a young man, brought back memories of the days when they were young.

When he was courting her, he had taken her on a late afternoon ride to a picturesque overlook. They both sat quietly, enjoying the scenic view, which reminded Karoline of a layer cake: first a line of green spruce trees, then the large buildings and houses of Kristiana, and finally the outer layer of the cake being the blue, cold water.

Karoline could sense Kristoffer's nervousness, and to assure him, she had gently laid her hand on top of his. She said nothing but sat and continued to stare ahead, allowing her gentle pressure to calm him. He laid his other hand on top of hers, and without looking directly at her, he said, "I would be honored if you would be my wife."

His proposal wasn't the overly romantic, grand gesture she'd expected. No wild abandonment of his feelings. No oaths of eternal love. His affection for her seemed to be more quiet and solid.

Her simple "yes" made Kristoffer smile, and that made her smile along with him. After she had given her consent, he requested permission from her parents. They had said that she could only marry after she turned eighteen. He agreed to their request, and they married in the Lutheran church several weeks after her birthday, leaving the following month for America.

Twenty-two years in this new country slid by, filled with raising children, helping on the farm, celebrating births, and mourning deaths. Picnics, church auctions, quilting bees, dances—these were the things which had marked her years. Washing dishes, washing clothes, baking, cooking, scrubbing, gardening, canning—these were the chores that marked her weeks. The days added to weeks, which added to months, which added to years.

At forty, she considered herself an old woman. Her hair had started to turn grey in her thirties; now, there was little left of its rich auburn color though she still wore it plaited in a crown. Her skin, wrinkled by days working outside either in the garden or in the field with Kristoffer, was also rough and mottled with sunspots. Her hands—calloused and wrinkled from pulling weeds, scrubbing clothes, and washing dishes—looked like those of an eighty-year-old woman. Her fingers were gnarled with arthritis. They certainly did not look like the hands of the young woman who had taken Kristoffer's in marriage.

Karoline, drawn back to the present, felt the discomfort of oppressive heat and humidity. The temperature had risen to ninety degrees, pairing with high humidity, which lay on her skin and crawled down into her lungs, making it difficult to get enough air. Moisture from her overheated skin flowed down her back and chest and underarms. The collar of her dress, soaked by her sweat, chafed around her throat, and her hands had swollen and felt tight in her riding gloves. Her throat was parched, and she wished for a glass of cold water.

She could see the water from the ice blocks dripping onto the ground when she last stopped to rest the horses. The man at the Cedar Falls Icehouse had cautioned her that the ice might not make it the entire way to Soldier. She needed to find another icehouse to replenish. There was one in Des Moines, but she was taking a northern route, and that would be many miles out of her way. The local ice sellers would not have the large blocks needed to travel longer distances, or they had their own customers to provision and wouldn't want to sell all of their stock. She was told there would probably be an icehouse in Ames along the Des Moines River. What would she do if she couldn't replenish the ice?

This was exactly the condition of her marriage: trouble came, and Kristoffer was not there to help her. While it was not his fault this time, it had been so many times in the past. He would leave with good intentions, but something that was too much for her to solve on her own would arrive like an uninvited and unwelcome guest. She was sometimes forced to rely on perfect strangers to help her instead of the one who was bound by God and the promise he had made to her father. Sometimes, when she did her best to solve whatever came through her door, Kristoffer was angry with her. Either she had made the wrong decision or she had made a decision without him. It felt to her that she could never please him. Karoline felt like a constant disappointment. What would he think about her going by herself to retrieve his body? She could hear his answer in her head. She could hear him berate her for traveling alone, for not thinking about the melting ice.

Even in death, Kristoffer could make her feel inadequate. As she usually did, Karoline fought back. Why did he have to die so far away? Why were things always her fault?

Thinking of the past brought back that familiar slow anger that grew within her when she felt that he had let her down. As her husband, she felt it was his duty to make sure that she was safe and well cared for. Now, he had left her with a farm that needed constant work and his children to rear on her own. Feeling guilty for thinking ill of the dead, Karoline bundled up her emotions, stored them somewhere in the recesses of her mind, and focused on their children.

1884

Seven and a half months pregnant, Karoline's small frame could barely move. Her stomach had expanded so voluminously that she could no longer see her feet or anything within a six-inch perimeter around them. Her back often ached from the added weight, and today it seemed to bother her more than others. The temperature had dropped, and they were expecting a spring snowstorm. She wondered whether this atmospheric pressure change had caused these more intense aches.

Minnesota's late winter storms were not uncommon. She didn't mind Minnesota, but they had never discussed living there. Karoline discovered on their trip over the Atlantic that Kristoffer didn't have enough money to buy a farm at that time and hadn't made firm plans for their living. She discovered this by overhearing a conversation between him and another man.

"I had hoped to have saved more money," Kristoffer admitted to him.

"How short are you for a farm?" the stranger questioned.

"I only had enough for the passage and train tickets as far as the Middle West."

"What are your plans after that?" Karoline could hear the disbelief in the man's question.

"I don't know," admitted Kristoffer. "I figured something would come up once we arrived in America. And since there is farmland in the Middle West, there will be farm work. I can always do that for a while until I get enough money to buy my own farm."

She was stunned that she hadn't been told the truth of their situation. He had misrepresented himself in order to convince her to go to America with him. Had she known that they weren't completely secure in their move, she might have declined to go right away, preferring to continue living with her parents until he had earned enough money to send for her. Throughout the rest of the trip, she couldn't shake her shock and disappointment.

On their journey from New York to the Middle West, Kristoffer met many other Norwegian families traveling to Minnesota. Minneapolis and St. Paul, major logging towns, brought a large number of immigrants to work in the logging business. Because of its similar climate to Norway and other Nordic countries, many of the original settlers in that area had encouraged their relatives to come and make money. Kristoffer decided to change from their Iowa destination, which was uncertain as far as ready work, to Minnesota, which advertised jobs in the paper. Since Karoline didn't know America's territory, one state over another didn't really matter to her. She was hurt that he hadn't decided to include her in the decision-making. She started to feel more like his child than his wife.

Kristoffer easily obtained a job cutting down trees. The logging company provided lodging in large, roomy tents. He would also be provided with meals. Kristoffer was grateful to get his logging job. Because it was too far from their living quarters and the loggers went farther into the forest each day, he came home every other weekend, leaving Karoline alone, and loneliness grew each day. She counted the days until his return and counted again when he had to leave. She felt isolated in this new country. She didn't speak the language, she didn't know anyone, and she didn't know anything about her surroundings. She felt trapped by her own ignorance. At times, though, she felt guilty for being disappointed by the amount of time he spent away from her. If they were to buy their dream farm, he would have to work enough to save the money. Unless he spent time at the logging camp, they would never have enough.

As soon as they arrived in St. Paul, they sought affordable housing. Karoline imagined a small wooden house, but since they had no immediate means, they were relegated to taking what they could find with the money they had, which was a house dug out of a side of a hill, four miles from St. Paul. It had a door and a single window. The ceiling of the dugout was shorter than Kristoffer's six-foot frame. He remained stooped from the minute he stepped into the door until he either sat or lay down. Karoline was more fortunate in that her shorter stature didn't require any bending to walk around. Otherwise, her indoor chores would have been impossible in her condition.

She had to admit that the dugout was warmer in the winter than the wooden houses she had visited. In those houses, the wind stole through the cracks and slithered down her neck. Their residents were never completely warm until the summer months arrived. Other than its warmth, her lodging left little else to brag about. There was limited space inside, fitting only their bed, their traveling chest, a dresser for clothes, a shelf for dishes, and a place to keep water for washing. With a dirt floor and walls, her living quarters never felt clean. Kristoffer had whitewashed the walls to brighten them, but they still crumbled, which left patches of dark mixed in with the white. Bugs seemed to be permanent residents, and after the first three months, she stopped trying to exterminate them. Worse than the bugs was the never-ending damp. It sat in her lungs, and at the worst times, her ragged cough stole her breath, leaving her crouched over in a chair trying to revive her lungs.

She had suggested that they move into a better home as soon as they had enough money to sustain them for the rent, but Kristoffer had pointed out that they could save even more money if they stayed in the dugout. The expense was less than half of what a wooden house would have cost. While he was very pragmatic and thrifty, two characteristics she had admired in her own father, Kristoffer wasn't the one who spent the most time in the dugout.

When he came home to her, he was exuberant and full of stories from his work companions. He had formed a friendship with the Svensen brothers, a pair of bachelor Norwegians who loved cards and gambling and drink. Karoline did not approve of any of these activities, but Kristoffer assured her that he did not gamble when he played cards. He knew how important their money was to her and their imminent newborn. She often felt that he would rather be with his friends in the logging camp than with her.

With no friends of her own, she had no one to ask about the pro-gression of marriage. Was it normal for men to be less attentive to their wives once they married? How long into a marriage (theirs was only a little over a year old) before the husband preferred the com-pany of friends to his wife? With no other woman to confide in, she could only speculate for herself why he seemed to prefer male com-pany to hers. She had begun to doubt herself and her ability to be a good wife.

She also had no friend to ask for pregnancy advice. If she had been in Norway, her mother would have brought her through the first pregnancy with a calm, expert hand. Instead, Karoline was left to wonder about the changes in her body as they came along. As her belly swelled, she began to anticipate the birth, especially how she would accomplish delivery should Kristoffer be at the camp, which seemed likely. Could she send for a doctor? What other help was there for her? While these questions formed in the back of her mind, she was able to put them off. She still had many weeks to figure out the details, and Kristoffer would be back several times before then, which gave her a chance to form plans with him since he knew more of the community of loggers' wives. She knew no one well enough to ask for help. And fears were beginning to build in her mind when she thought about all of the things that could go wrong while she was giving birth. With no husband or woman friend to confide in about all of her doubts and fears, she felt no better off than a solitary animal burrowed away.

Allowing her mind to return to immediate concerns, Karoline felt her back ache deeper and more intensely. She tried to find more comfortable positions: sitting straight on a Windsor back chair, lying down on their bed and on the floor. However, no position seemed to relieve her. She walked around the dugout in small circles because there was no room, and the outdoor weather was too poor for her comfort. She lay down on her side with no relief, so she moved to her back with no relief, and then returned to her side. She used a wooden spoon to rub into the painful spot. Nothing worked. Consequently, she went about the rest of her daily chores to distract her mind from concentrating on the pain, yet a squeezing came and went across the front of her stomach, accompanied by a dull ache.

She waited expectantly for Kristoffer to walk in through the door. It was one of his weekends home. As his expected arrival time drew closer, she looked outside to see whether his form had appeared somewhere in the distance. The last couple of times she looked out, the snow had changed from light flakes to large, fluffy ones that started to limit her vision across the yard. When he did arrive, she planned to send him right back out to fetch a doctor from town. Of all of the changes her body had gone through so far, nothing had brought this kind of pain. She was starting to worry that something was wrong.

As her worry grew inside of her, her imagination took off like a runaway horse. Her mind's eye could envision a dead child inside of her. That same eye pictured her body squeezing her child until it suffocated. In times of fear, she always went to the extreme. It became real to her. In the past, when her father had missed his supper, she was positive that he had been thrown from the horse, had hit his head on a rock, and was lying out in a field somewhere, bleeding to death. But when he walked through the door, the worry drained from her. He had wanted to finish the planting and stayed out until the last seed was in the dirt.

Another squeeze brought her back to her own problem. Time passed, and now she knew absolutely that there was something wrong. She looked out one more time and could not see fifty feet in front of her face. The storm had created a whiteout, and Kristoffer's tardiness was now explained. At that moment, she felt a trickle of water run down her leg. She knew she had not released her bladder. In all of the times she had attended her mother's quilting circle, she heard the women mention "breaking waters." That was then followed by "labor," which she knew meant baby. Panic saturated every part of her body. She could not have this baby by herself. What if she died in childbirth? Other women in her church had suffered that fate after a long, grueling labor. She was not due for another six or eight weeks. Could this really be the baby coming? Or was it something much worse?

Karoline started to take deep, calming breaths. Her mother had modeled for her how to stay calm in the face of something horrible. She had made Karoline breathe with her and think aloud what needed to be done. Karoline started to make a mental list of supplies and gathered them as she thought of them: blankets, clean sheets, twine, scissors, a pan of water. She laid them all on a table next to their bed.

She began walking again, breathing. However, as she thought of her mother and her absent husband, she began to get angry, and when she got angry she always started to cry.

"Where are you? Where ARE you?" she screamed to the walls. "I hate this dugout. I hate you. And I miss my mother! You promised my parents you would protect me. You told my father you would never leave me. You told my mother you would keep me safe."

The door opened, and a snow-laden Kristoffer came stamping in. His collar was pulled up around his ears, and his pants had snow clinging to them up to his knees. When he looked up and saw Karoline's face, red and swollen from crying, he immediately went to her.

"What is wrong? Are you hurt? What happened?" he asked without taking a pause to allow her to answer.

"The baby is coming. I need help. You need to get a doctor... Now!"

"I can't," he cried. "The storm is too terrible. No doctor would go out into this weather even if I could reach his house. I don't even know where one lives. I didn't have time to ask the women."

"Then you'll have to help me. I don't know exactly what to do, but we don't have a choice."

"I can't!" he screamed.

"You will, or you will find another way. This baby is coming, and I'm not doing it alone. You brought me here away from my mother, so you are responsible for helping me."

"I will get the neighbor lady. She has children and most certainly knows what to do."

"What about the storm? How will you not get lost?"

"I will make sure to bring her back. Let me worry about how. Do you think you can wait an hour or two? Do you feel like it's coming now?"

"I don't think it's coming now," she replied. "My mother once told me that the first baby always takes more time."

With those words, Kristoffer put a load of wood into the fireplace to build up the light inside the dugout. He also put one of their lanterns in the window and hoped he could make it to the neighbors' house and back. He then went outside and tied a rope between their dugout and the tree at the end of their lane. From their lane's end, it was a straight shot. If he ran most of the way there, he thought that he could make it in a little less than an hour. It would take longer getting back because he could not expect that neighbor lady to run with him.

Karoline lost track of the time. A few minutes seemed like an hour. To her, it felt like he had been gone for four or five. At some point in the wait, she had started labor contractions. She wasn't sure what she was supposed to do. Should she lie down? Continue to walk around? What if the baby came before he returned? Could she deliver on her own? She supposed women had done this on their own before her. Women had been birthing children since the beginning of time. She was certain of one fact: this baby would arrive whether or not the neighbor woman came to help, or whether she was standing up or lying down. She eventually decided to stay in a flat position on the bed. Her back hurt her so much that it seemed the best course of action to relieve as much of the pain as she could.

She started to feel hard contractions closer together. At one point, she felt an intense pressure and felt like she wanted to push.

With a gush of cold air, the door flew open and a snow-covered Kristoffer and the neighbor woman came through the doorway. Lena Andersen—a tall, blonde Swede—had a husband who also worked in the logging camp. She had never met Karoline but knew there was a woman living in the dugout. With her own children to keep her busy, she hadn't made time to travel the distance to say hello properly.

"Hello, Karoline. I'm Lena, and I'm here to help you. Don't you worry none. All of us logging women have been helping each other deliver our babies. The doctor won't come around here anyway. He said that he won't touch unhygienic logging women. You're better off without him. Now let's see what's what here."

Lena lifted Karoline's skirt and peered under. "Oh, my," she said. "Your baby is planning to come out backwards. I'm glad I've arrived in time. You would have never got him out."

Lena took command of the house, telling Kristoffer to put water on to boil. She checked Karoline's birthing supplies on the stool and nodded her approval. "Okay, Karoline. It's too late to try to turn him, so I'm going to help you deliver him the way he is. I'm going to have you slide down to the edge of the bed. When he's part way out, I'm going to let him hang. The gravity will bring him the rest of the way. Now, with each contraction, you are going to push as hard as you can. Okay?"

Karoline nodded her assent and began the hard work. Lena encouraged her and gave her positive reinforcement. Kristoffer moved to the farthest corner of the dugout, and Karoline assumed that he was too queasy to see any blood or watch her go through her pain. While the small distance did not allay the screaming, he at least didn't have to look at his wife's burdensome labor and pain.

Finally, the baby's head slipped out. The newborn did not breathe until Lena cleared the airway and rubbed the body vigorously.

"It's not a he; it's a she." Lena, beaming at Karoline, held up the tiny girl. She was pink and wrinkled and bald.

Lena wrapped her in one of the blankets that Karoline had gathered and waited for the afterbirth. She told Karoline that she could rest for a while and hold her baby. It would not happen for at least half an hour.

Not more than fifteen minutes passed before Karoline started to experience pains again. Lena became concerned because the afterbirth usually slipped out without the mother noticing, which is why she wanted Karoline to focus on the baby.

The pains became so intense that Karoline handed the baby back to Lena. Lena put the baby in a dresser drawer and looked again under Karoline's sheet. She could see the crown of another baby.

"Karoline, you have another baby coming. I need you to gather all of your strength and push again."

"I can't," Karoline whimpered. "I'm too tired."

"If you can travel to this country and live in this dugout, you can do anything. Now, push."

The second baby came out head first and didn't take nearly as long. Karoline delivered a second girl. This one was also pink and wrinkled and bald, but she was smaller than the first one. Lena wrapped her in another blanket and handed her to Kristoffer.

"Two," he said. "How did we end up with two? How will we take care of two?"

Pragmatically, Lena replied, "Well, you can't return one. Whether you think you can or not, you'll have to. The loggers' wives will help look after your three girls."

"Thank you so much for taking care of me," Karoline said. "I couldn't have done this without you. You and I are now joined together like these girls." For the first time since moving to America, Karoline felt like she had a new Runa.

1885

From the deepest part of her lungs, Karoline howled like an injured animal. She sank down onto her knees and folded over onto the dirt floor with her head down and her arms wrapped over the top of her head. She rocked back and forth. She kept that position while wracking sobs exploded from the bottom of her soul. She then grabbed her hair and pulled it out in chunks while she continued to wail.

Her babies, Ingrid and Inger, always slept nestled together in the crib. Now fourteen months old, they usually made it through the night without waking. Each morning at 5:30, Karoline put her face down into the crib and kissed each baby awake.

Lena, carrying a breakfast apple tart to Karoline's dugout, could hear a baby wailing as well as low animal sounds. Lena rushed into the dugout and saw Karoline sitting on the floor with a baby in her lap. Ingrid lay in the crib, crying from hunger. Lena knelt down next to Karoline and took the baby from her. Inger, who had been wheezing with each breath, was now silent and cold. And dead.

Ingrid and Inger had battled lung problems from the very beginning. Their premature births had stolen away those last few weeks when their lungs would have finished developing. Inger often sounded as though she was panting while she was trying to draw breath. At times, her small fingernails and lips had a tinge of blue. Ingrid, who was stronger, could still easily develop a cough. Lena told Karoline that the babies would grow, eventually developing strong enough lungs to make them completely healthy.

The damp of the dugout, however, only added to their health issues. In the spring, rains fell consistently, making the dugout air humid. Inger caught a chest cold and barked with a rheumy cough all through the month of April. No poultice seemed to relieve her congested lungs. Lena had reached out to the other logging women for their home remedies, which Karoline tried, but to no avail. Inger grew worse each day.

Karoline, avoiding sleep, listened to her tiny daughter fight for each breath through the long nights. After a busy day of household chores, sometimes it was difficult to stay awake. Her eyes felt so heavy. Sometimes she closed just one of them to rest a little, but eventually both would drop down. Something she heard or dreamt would startle her awake. The long nights of worry and guilt over falling asleep wore on Karoline. She felt it unfair that she was alone once again to solve this problem.

After their birth, Kristoffer had begun making the long walk home every weekend because he couldn't stand to be away from his new babies. As soon as he walked in the door, he would give Karoline some gift he had found along the way: a bunch of wild flowers, an interesting rock, or a plant he thought would look nice in front of the dugout. Once he kissed his wife, he scooped up both babies, one in each arm, and sang Norwegian lullabies to them. He told them stories about their family and imagined young men who would come to court them. He said, "They'll have to get by me first," looking at Karoline with a grin on his face.

The twins were perfect copies of each other, having their father's dark hair and bright blue eyes. However, they had their mother's alabaster skin. Their tiny fingers and toes were perfect. They had identical heart-shaped mouths with beautiful shell-pink lips.

Karoline had never been happier than during those first few months of the girls' lives. She felt closer to her husband and could hardly describe the passion she felt for him. She missed him when he was gone and felt such strong misery when he walked out the door. She had a perfect husband. She had perfect children. They had a perfect family.

When the twins were four months old, Kristoffer announced to Karoline, "I'm not going to come home every week. Walking is wearing out my shoes, and I've been missing any extra work that becomes available on the weekends. I'm losing potential extra money—money we need."

Her heart tore, but she had to admit that they were in need. The two additional family members would soon become more expensive as they outgrew their second-hand clothing and started eating solid food instead of breast milk. She would miss him; however, she consoled herself that it would not be like before. Kristoffer would be a loving husband and father when he returned, and she now had connections to other women and wouldn't feel as lonely. Karoline had established a permanent bond with Lena, who introduced her to other logging mothers. These kind women brought over outgrown, hand-me-down clothes for the girls as well as other baby necessities. Lena would often look in on Karoline, bringing some kind of Swedish baked goods. Karoline started to feel like America was becoming her home.

In Kristoffer's long absences, her relationship with him returned to its previous condition. He went back to his bi-weekly returns and relayed stories of the Svensen brothers. He was less rapt with the babies the longer he was around them. They cried often, and he wasn't interested in changing clouts. On one of the weekends, he told her he was going to the Svensen brothers' house to play cards with them. She felt it was not her place to tell him what he could do with his time, but she thought he should stay at home with his family when he returned to them.

Since all of the child and house care fell to Karoline, she began to resent his being gone so often. The dugout was no place to raise children. To grow healthy and strong, the girls needed a clean atmosphere, sunshine, and crisp air. When she asked Kristoffer if they could rent a wooden house, maybe one closer to the other logging women, he reminded her again of the money they were saving with such cheap rent. Karoline lashed back at him.

"I hate this dugout! I feel like I'm living like an animal. We are always dirty and damp. I can't keep anything clean."

"As the man, I make the decisions, and I have decided that we will continue to live here. I am the one who makes the money. As my wife, you'll do as I say."

"The head of the family would put his children's welfare ahead of everything else. If you were my father, you would not have us living in this filth!" In comparing him to her father, Karoline had gone too far. She knew her last statement would hurt him, which was what she intended.

But instead of speaking back, Kristoffer walked out the door. He did not return that weekend, and she assumed he had gone to sleep on the Svensen brothers' floor. She would not see him for another two weeks. She was both sorry and glad to see him go. She had meant to make him remember the promise he had made to her parents.

The first few days of the first week he was gone were like any other. Karoline fed children, cooked food, washed laundry, mended clothes, and completed a hundred other chores that made her weekly list. The laundry was especially burdensome. When the girls were small, their clouts took less time to soak, scrub, and hang on the line. Now that they were eating cereals, they took more time and more work. The girls had also started to crawl, needing more vigilance from Karoline. When she dropped into bed at night, she was instantly asleep, exhausted from her daily activities. She no longer tried to stay awake through the night to listen to their breathing.

By the fourth day he was gone, Inger's breathing became worse. Lena brought two women over to the dugout to help diagnose the little girl. Inger's wheezing and barking alarmed them. They were fairly certain that she had pneumonia. All of the women had a lengthy discussion about the best course of action. They agreed that the dugout was bad for Inger's health. One of the women, a large German named Alice, offered to take Inger to her wooden house to take care of her. Agnes, a petite blonde Norwegian who reminded Karoline of Runa, said they should take Inger to the doctor. Karoline wished she could have asked her mother for advice. She would have known how to make Inger better. She even wished she could consult with Kristoffer, not that he had any medical knowledge, but his daughter's life rested in her hands alone.

She thanked Alice for her offer, but Karoline was too proud to take charity. She noticed that Alice hadn't offered to take Karoline or Ingrid. If Inger became worse, Karoline would have to take Ingrid with her to go to Alice's house. What if she didn't make it in time? What if Ingrid got sick, being out in the middle of the night? Mostly, Karoline didn't want to be away from her baby.

Karoline wanted to take Inger to the doctor. Kristoffer never left money with her, only store credit for her to buy their necessities. He had a box with money buried next to the dugout, but it was not to be used for anything but the purchase of the farm. As well, the doctor lived in St. Paul, and it would take time to walk the distance. She wasn't sure whether that would make Inger worse. She was also assuming the doctor would let her pay her bill when Kristoffer returned. When Lena had come to help deliver the twins, she also mentioned that the doctor didn't like healing the loggers and their wives. She might walk all that way only for him to shut his door to her.

After her deliberations, Karoline thanked the women for their concern. She had decided she would keep Inger with her and would continue the poultices to see if she could loosen up the baby's chest.

Nothing seemed to work on Inger. Each day and each night, Karoline could barely breathe as she listened to her daughter. Inger cried constantly, gulping for air. Ingrid cried because her sister cried. Karoline could only hold her babies in her arms and walk around the dugout. The laundry piled in a corner. The dirty, crusted dishes were stacked on the table. Not even their bodies were bathed.

Each hour with each day brought more resentment. She could imagine Kristoffer gathered around a table in the tent, playing cards with his friends—laughing, joking, smoking their pipes. His only concern would be the time it would take him to get to the outhouse. Someone else was making sure he ate well. Someone else cleaned up his dishes. And he would expect her to clean his clothes when he returned. Did he even think about her, she wondered? Did he miss her? Did he miss their children? Did he worry about them? Was he even concerned about the health of their babies?

Lena took Inger's tiny body and wrapped it in one of Karoline's best tablecloths and took the body to a cool cellar. Karoline had carried that cloth with her across an ocean, halfway across a continent. It was part of her hope chest, the one she had started when she was nine years old. She had embroidered tiny, blue forget-me-not flowers around the perimeter. The irony of the embroidery struck her. The forget-me-nots were meant for her husband, who—in her opinion—had forgotten all about them. Now, they were meant for the child she would never forget.

Karoline, at first, blamed herself. She replayed the conversation with the women. If she had given Inger to Alice, would Inger still be alive? Her own pride and selfishness had killed her child. God was punishing her pride. Her agony was her penance. When Kristoffer came home, what would he say? Would he blame her, too?

At the end of the second week, Kristoffer walked through the door. The dugout's condition was the first sign that something was wrong. Dirty dishes and clothing were stacked around, nothing had been picked up, and the bed was not made. Karoline, an excellent housekeeper, would never abide by these slovenly ways. As he moved farther into the dugout, he could see her lying in the bed with the covers up around her shoulder. He assumed the girls must be in there with her because they were nowhere else. "Karoline? What's wrong? Are you sick?"

Karoline didn't respond. Ingrid, awakened by her father's voice, popped her head up and said, "*Fadir*."

"Karoline! Answer me. Are you ill? What's wrong?"
Karoline, holding Ingrid in her arms, sat up in bed. She stared into Kristoffer's face without expression. She had no feelings left. They had drained from her drop by drop. "Inger is dead."

"What do you mean by dead? Why dead? How dead?"

"This dugout killed her. Her breathing. She caught pneumonia and couldn't breathe. Three days ago, I went to their crib, and Inger had died in the night. I could do nothing. She was already cold. If she had had a better home, she would be alive right now. If you had let us move, she would still be alive!"

Stunned, Kristoffer stared blankly back at her. After a minute, tears began sliding down his cheeks into his beard. "Oh, Karoline, I'm so sorry. I wish I had been here. I wish I had known sooner. Where is she?"

"Lena took her. She said she would take care of her. You need to build a coffin, so we can bury her. Lena has already found us a Lutheran minister. I wish I could take her back to Norway to be buried in our family's cemetery plot. We have no choice but to bury her here in St. Paul." Although she didn't think she had any tears left, Karoline began to cry anew.

Karoline could see the irritation in the corners of his mouth. She realized why. She had given him commands. She had already made decisions and plans. But she didn't care if he was irritated with her for taking over, and his irritation sparked her anger. It served him right. If he was a proper father, he would have been there to save Inger. At the very least, he would have taken care of the funeral arrangements instead of leaving the neighbors to do it for his wife.

They held the funeral service on the following Monday. Apart from Karoline and Kristoffer, only Lena and a few other women attended. The logging men were at work, and Karoline had left Ingrid with Alice, the German woman. Karoline was afraid she would lose another baby if she brought her out in the elements. The service was short and simple. They had hired a minister who said some gravesite prayers. Karoline had insisted that the tablecloth stay with Inger. One of the women had given Karoline a dress for Inger, so she could be buried in something that looked nicer than her current outfits. The tablecloth was the nicest thing Karoline could leave with her daughter. It was also a part of Norway, so Inger would know her roots.

The mortician, his sons, and Kristoffer threw spade after spade of dirt onto the tiny coffin. With each shovel full of dirt, Karoline shed fresh tears. How could she leave her daughter's tiny body in that cold ground? Her mother's heart told her she needed to stay by Inger's side to protect her. When the burying was finished and the dirt mounded, Karoline lay down on the burial site and wept uncontrollably. Kristoffer was forced to pick her up. "Come, Karoline. We must go home now."

On the way home from the cemetery, Karoline said very little. She now put the blame of Inger's death on Kristoffer. It was his stubborn frugality that had caused their baby's death.

When they could finally sight their dugout, Karoline turned to Kristoffer. "We are going to move into a wood house. And I want this done by next week. I'm not going to lose another child."

"You don't make the decisions. I do. I've allowed you to play the head of the house for our daughter's funeral, but you won't be telling me what we will and will not do any longer. You'll do as I say. You'll abide by my decisions. And we will stay here. I will go back to the logging camp tomorrow. I can't afford to lose another day."

Karoline said nothing. Her face flushed red. She was not going to lose another child. She was not going to live like an animal. She was not going to stay with a man who couldn't think of his own family's welfare.

Kristoffer left at first light the next day. As soon as he was out the door, Karoline packed her chest, the one that she had brought to this forsaken place, with her and Ingrid's things. She took only what they needed, leaving behind household goods. She would ask one of the women who had a wagon to take her, the baby, and their chest to the railroad station. Before she walked out the door, she decided to leave Kristoffer a note, explaining her whereabouts in case he thought she had been kidnapped.

Kristoffer,

Jeg vil ikke leve som et dyr på dette stedet. Ingrid og jeg skal tilbake til Norge.

Din kone,
Karoline

Kristoffer,

I will not live like an animal in this place. Ingrid and I are going back to Norway.

Your wife,
Karoline

1905

Giving herself and the horses a much-needed break from the heat, Karoline pulled the wagon off the path near a grassy spot. She jumped down from the seat and let the reins slacken, giving the horses their independence to feed on the dandelions growing among the weeds. Karoline sat on the ground in the shade of the wagon and took off her boots. She put her hot feet into the cool vegetation. She leaned back against the wagon and dug her toes further into the greens. The contrast of the heat and the cool gave her immense pleasure.

She remembered when she and Kristoffer were courting, and he had taken her to a small pond near her family's farm on one of their earlier outings. The heat of the summer had come on, and the day was clear with a slight breeze. She had packed a picnic lunch for the two of them: bread, herring, strawberries, and her mother's goat cheese. Before they ate, they had both pulled off their boots and dipped their feet into the refreshing water. He pretended to be shocked by her large feet, and she pretended to be offended. She told him that he could have none of her picnic wares, and he promised never to mention her feet again if she would share with him. After their jovial ribbing, they fell into a long silence, both staring into the water. Karoline thought about the courtship and where it would take them. She hoped for a marriage proposal. She wondered if he felt the same. Was he thinking about her as he sat there?

The couple revisited the pond several times. Their first kiss happened at that pond. He had reached over, she thought, to put a flower—a snow buttercup—in her hair, but instead of slipping the stem of the white puff into her thick tresses, he stroked her cheek with the flower and moved close to her face, taking her chin as he brought his mouth to hers. After he pulled away, she decided she wanted no other man to put his lips against hers.

With her eyes closed and the coolness surrounding her feet, Karoline could resurface the feeling of that long-ago kiss. She had been excited to be with this man. He made her feel happy and carefree. Her whole body seemed to permanently vibrate, giddiness flowing through her when she even thought about him.

Why had it changed? Had she done something that changed his feelings about her? Had something happened to him to take away that humor and bravado?

After they married, the farther they had sailed away from Norway, the more business-like and domineering Kristoffer had become. He had begun guiding her not with a gentle hand on her back but more of a shove from behind. He'd also snapped at her and often pointed when he wanted her to do something. Instead of including her in any conversation, he talked about her while she was standing right there. And once they stepped onto American soil, his persona had grown serious and terse. She'd begun to succumb to his moods, retreating further into herself, afraid to provoke his ire.

Karoline was used to her mother deferring to her father's wishes, but he'd spoken to his wife when decisions needed to be made. She had never seen her father boss her mother. He certainly had never snapped at her like a dog. She had wrongly assumed that all marriages were like theirs.

At first, when Kristoffer was abrupt and bossy, she'd felt devastated and had cried quietly where he could not see her. Soon after, he would do something thoughtful, like pick wildflowers for her or rub her tired feet. He knew he had hurt her feelings and wanted to make amends. Each bark or command made another hole in her heart, and instead of a solid mass, it had become a cheesecloth. Kristoffer eventually quit trying to make amends and grew irritated with her crying. She knew that if she took every harsh word to heart, she would have no heart left. She worked on dismissing his gruffness with silence. While she wanted to forget his slights, she could not. Instead, they built up inside of her, replacing that newly married love. She didn't like it, but she would not survive if every cut needed tending. She would instead allow calluses to grow over them.

As a good wife should, she had obeyed him in all commands and followed his every decision, except the one. Now, even at forty years old, she was still surprised at her own spunk when she had packed up her baby and herself and taken them back to Norway.

1885

When Karoline decided to leave for Norway, taking Ingrid with her, she broke her vow of obedience. She was putting the life of her child before her wedding vow. And she didn't care. Her anger gave her strength and fearlessness. Once again, though, she needed Lena's help. She had no transportation, and she couldn't walk with a baby and a large chest. She found Lena out feeding her chickens. "Lena, I need some help from you. Do you know someone who could use their wagon and take me to the train station in St. Paul?"

"*Ja*. I think I can find someone. Why are you going to the train?"

"I'm going back to Norway."

"What? Why? Did he hit you?"

"No. But I'm not living in that anthill any longer. He won't let us move, and I won't lose this baby. So I'm going home."

"All the way to Norway? By yourself? How will you pay for it?"

"I dug up his money box and took what I needed for the train trip."

"Where will you stay before you board the ship? How will you pay for your passage? And you're pregnant again, *ja*? And you're still going to leave?"

"I have to. I'm going to do better by Ingrid and this new baby. I'll figure out the rest along the way."

Karoline did not know when the next ship for Norway would leave from New York. She would have to find a job for their passage, and she did not have the financial means to stay in a boarding house until the departure. Instead of New York, she bought a ticket to Chicago. Her sister Sophie had also made the trip to America six months after Karoline, making her home in that large Middle Western city. She had secured a position as a nanny for a widowed lawyer named Glen Johnson and his two young boys. Not even a year had passed before Sophie's stunning beauty and charm had brought her and Glen to the altar. She now lived a comfortable life.

Karoline would be able to stay with Sophie and her husband until such time as she could take another train from Chicago to New York, boarding the ship to Norway. Karoline had faith that her sister would either supply the money needed for both train and boat passage or find her a job so that she could earn the money for herself.

She had wired Sophie at the St. Paul train station; consequently, there was a horse and driver waiting for them when they stepped down from the train. As they pulled up to Sophie's house, Karoline's eyes grew wide, and her mouth opened a little. The house was a grey, stone Victorian mansion with a large front lawn. A long, matching stone sidewalk led to a front porch that stretched across the length of the house. She counted three stories with a cupola on one side. The second story also included a porch, and she could see at least six gables. She had never seen such a spectacular building. Karoline speculated that at least ten of her dugouts could fit inside this monster house.

When she stepped up to Sophie's door, she and Ingrid were greeted with tears and kisses. Karoline put down her luggage, wrapped her arms around her sister, and allowed her own tears to come. Sophie, suffering from homesickness, reciprocated the embrace—the two of them standing on the porch, crying from homesickness. Sophie then reached out for Ingrid, took her niece in her arms, and inhaled her scent. Sophie could have no children of her own. Excited, she rattled off the cultural events they might want to attend in the city, the picnics they could have in the park, and new restaurants where they could dine.

After allowing Karoline a few days of rest, Sophie commented that Karoline seemed to be thicker around the middle. "Yes," Karoline said. "I think I am about five and a half months pregnant."

"You're going to Norway to have this new child? What will Kristoffer think?"

"Right now, I don't care what he thinks. I'm better off having this child in Norway. Mother can help me deliver it, and the baby and Ingrid will have better living conditions. I was too ashamed to tell the family that we were living in a dugout."

Karoline relayed to Sophie the grueling birth of the twins and the soul-shattering story of Inger's death. She sobbed all over again, this time with someone who knew her well and loved her unconditionally. As she poured forth her stories, Sophie put her arm around Karoline's shoulder, stroking her head and cheek to comfort her. Karoline had not felt comfort this sympathetic since she'd last seen her mother. She realized how much she had been holding in her own grief. She had had to continue with her daily chores and provide for Ingrid. She had kept her mind on her tasks and had tried to shut out thoughts of Inger. Now, with someone else to look after them, she could grieve.

During their three-month stay, Karoline and Ingrid grew healthy under Sophie's care. Ingrid's lungs cleared up, and she ceased coughing. Their cheeks grew pink, and they both put on some weight. Sophie made sure to give them the best food and rooms with the most sunshine. Karoline spent her days playing with her daughter and reminiscing with her sister. She began to feel like herself and finally was in the frame of mind to contemplate her marriage. Had she married the wrong man? Did she still love him? Would she eventually go back to him or stay in Norway? She felt like she needed the time and distance to find the answers to these questions. If she had to answer them now, she would say she had no feelings for him and would not be returning to him.

The ship's departure date from New York's harbor was September 26. Karoline would need to take another train, find a room to rent in New York, and purchase passage tickets. She had never done anything like this on her own. Someone had always led the way, first her father, then her husband. This time, she was the parent, leading a daughter, who had complete faith in her. Her very pregnant body made these responsibilities more difficult. Karoline knew she must be close to her delivery time, but she was resolute that she would have this new baby under her mother's roof.

On September 25, Karoline, having made it to New York, purchased third-class tickets for both her and Ingrid, compliments of her brother-in-law, Glen. The steerage compartments were small with an upper and lower bunk on each side of the cabin, accommodating four people. A toilet and sink stood in the front of the room. The cabins were clean and neat, much nicer than the passage accommodations for immigrants before steam ships. Those new Americans had had to suffer through months of filth, disease, and poor food.

On the afternoon of September 26, Karoline and Ingrid boarded the *Thingvalla*. They would sail on a mild fall day with plenty of sunshine. Karoline could hardly believe that she was going home, her spirits lifting like a shining, white seagull. In a matter of days, her mother's arms would be wrapped around her, and all would be well again.

1905

Karoline's second passage on the *Thingvalla* was a month shy of twenty years ago, but it seemed like it had been more than a life-time. She thought about in what ways she was different from the Karoline who had made the trip to America and the one who had made the trip away from it.

On her first passage, she had clung to Kristoffer, allowing him to speak for them and make all of their decisions. She had even been afraid to speak to other passengers. When she made the trip back to Norway, it was after spending two years in America, struggling mostly by herself, which had forged her own passage into the woman she was today. She had turned strangers into friends and had asked for help when she needed it. She had made a trip halfway across a continent without Kristoffer's help. She had figured out how to purchase her own tickets and find the correct wharf for boarding the ship. She had even begun to think about being without Kristoffer because she could clearly take care of herself and her child.

Traveling without a man to Norway drew no suspicion from the other passengers, especially not the women. Many families returned to visit relatives after spending several years in America. Single women with children were not unusual since passage was expensive and a man would lose his job if he took time off. The husband could continue working while the wife spent months visiting her family.

Three days into the crossing, her newfound strength and independence was put to the test. Sometime in the night, she started to feel like a strong hand was wrenching and tightening its grip on her uterus. This time, she recognized the feel of labor and sought out help from some of the other female passengers. The other women were eager to help her and gathered the necessary supplies. One woman offered to take Ingrid back to her cabin and tuck her back into a bed. Two other women sat at her head, wiping her brow and holding her hand. Another woman, well experienced in childbirth with her own seven children, served as midwife and coached her through the process. All of them stayed beside her until her final push. This time, the baby was in the correct position and emerged with much less drama. Karoline had given birth to a little boy.

The women had asked her if she was going to name him after his father, especially since he was the first boy. Of course, she considered it, but only briefly. She named him Tingvald Atlantic after the ship and ocean. Instead of a hard c on Atlantic, she pronounced it with an s. At that time, she didn't know if she would return to Kristoffer. Instead of reminding her of her husband, Tingvald's name reminded her of the first time she had made her own way.

Now a widow, she would have to make her own way for the rest of her life. Her children would always be there if she needed help, but that mother-child relationship would keep her from relying on them. She was the stone in the river, the one they could reach for when they were swirling with difficulties.

A glance back into the wagon gave her mixed feelings. Part of her felt as cold as the ice covering his body. She could only think about how satisfied she felt in taking care of herself. Had she been unknowingly preparing for his death? Her trip to Norway and eventually back had permanently changed Karoline. She had morphed from a weak, dependent woman to a strong, independent one. After that trip, she considered herself an equal partner, not a frail wife. As a result, she often gave her opinions on matters, which irritated him. She also became more self-sufficient. She did not wait for him to fix a broken window. She pulled out her collection of house tools, which she had put together by herself, and replaced the pane.

Kristoffer didn't understand why she had become a completely different wife. The more he tried to assert his dominance over her, the more she pushed back against it. He resented her independence, and she ignored that resentment. Instead of asking for permission to make decisions regarding the household or the children, she acted first and informed later. The result was a fissure that grew into a gap that widened into a divide.

As she thought back upon her marriage and her own changes, she knew why she had become this way. She had done it to protect herself. Being dependent on him made her weak, thereby creating a heart that could easily be hurt. It was safer to put her love into her children and create a cordial, working relationship with her husband. They weren't the only couple who did not love each other.

The other part of her thought back to that dance and the kiss at the pond. She had felt deeply for him once. She had to give him credit for being a good provider for her and their children. For most women, this would have been enough. Why had she thought her marriage would be more? What had made her believe it should be filled with passionate love?

These were questions to consider for another time. Now, she had to think about her most pressing problem, the melting ice. Like Hansel and Gretel, she was leaving a trail, except hers was water. It was not the occasional drip, drip; it had become more of a steady stream. The Iowa heat was melting it at a worrying rate. And if the ice continued to melt at that rate, she would have a decomposing corpse in the back of her wagon.

1885

When Karoline and Ingrid walked down the gangplank, her father was waiting for her. Sophie had sent a telegram, informing her family of her arrival date. When her father saw Karoline with a swaddled baby, his face registered complete shock: he was expecting a small girl and a round belly.

As soon as Karoline stepped onto Norwegian soil, she felt awash in familiarity: the smell of land and water, familiar trees, familiar language from every person she saw. Being alone and foreign to her surroundings had created a tension in her entire body that she had not recognized until she could feel her muscles starting to relax. The sensation of coming back home was indescribable.

Her father wrapped his arms around his daughter and her baby and held them tight. He held onto them much longer than Karoline had ever experienced with him. When he picked up his granddaughter, he gave her a good squeeze and then stole a long moment to take in her face. Ingrid, wary of strangers, wiggled out of his arms.

Karoline leaned over and looked into Ingrid's eyes. She said, "This is your *farfar*. We will be staying with him and your *mormor* for a while. They live on a farm in a wooden house. Would you like to go see their house?" Ingrid, too shy to speak in front of a stranger, nodded her assent.

The wagon ride to the farm consisted of Karoline telling her father all about her life in America and the passage to Norway. She gave him general information about the birth on the ship. She also relayed news of Sophie and her husband. Karoline described their house and Sophie's stepsons. She then chatted about Lena and the other logging women. Karoline told her father how at home he would feel in Minnesota. The temperature and amount of snow were nearly identical. Both places were covered in spruce trees and had a great amount of water, though the type of fishing was very different. Minnesota had freshwater fish, so there were no sardines for Kristoffer's lunch. Amidst all of the news-giving and landscape-comparing, she did not mention Kristoffer or why she had returned home.

As soon as the wagon pulled onto the farm lane, Armaliea ran out of the house to meet them. Karoline and her children were yet again hugged and kissed. Her mother took Tingvald from Karoline's arms and carried him to the house. Karoline could feel her emotional burdens being left behind with each step she took toward her childhood home.

Her mother's kitchen smelled of cinnamon, cardamom, almond, apples, and fried dough. The fireplace infused the room with warmth, and the windows brought in sunshine. Her mother's kitchen was as bright and inviting as her dugout was dark and dank. Her mother's kitchen was clean and organized in maple cupboards; hers was dirty with cookware piled on wooden boards.

Armaliea had prepared a special dinner for her homecoming.

They ate ham glazed with apricot jelly and whiskey, fried potatoes and onions, baked rutabaga, and krumkakes with powdered sugar for dessert. Karoline had not eaten this well since her wedding dinner. Looking at the krumkakes brought back memories of those they had served at the church dance when she had met Kristoffer. She felt a small pang in her chest and wondered what he was doing and how angry he probably was with her, especially if he had discovered the missing money.

When they had all pushed back from the table, Karoline and her mother washed the dishes and cleaned the kitchen. Her father took both grandchildren into the parlor and showed them his violin. Karoline could hear them all laughing as he allowed Ingrid to pluck the strings of the instrument. She realized that Ingrid had not gotten such attention from a man. Ingrid's father was generally busy with chores when he came home, and she was tucked away in her blankets by the time he finished. Ingrid saw Kristoffer as the man who fixed things rather than the man who cherished and played with her.

Once the kitchen was spotless again, the whole family sat in front of the roaring fire in the parlor. Gulbran played a variety of Norwegian folk songs, and the family sang and danced to them. Ingrid's dark curls bounced as she clapped her chubby hands and stomped her tiny feet to the sound of the music. This was the first time she had heard music, and she was definitely her grandfather's girl because she was enthralled with it. Karoline realized how long it had been since her daughter had been so delighted. Their dugout wasn't a home like this one; it was a place of sadness and tears. Karoline wondered whether Ingrid could feel the tension between herself and Kristoffer.

Later that evening, Gulbran, Armaliea, and Karoline sat together. Her parents had waited until she was fed and her children settled before they asked why she was home.

"I left him. And I don't think that I'm going back to America."

She confessed all she had held back in her letters home: the dugout, the reason for Inger's death, her loneliness, and Kristoffer's refusal to move them to a proper home. Her mother cried, and her father remained silent, yet she could see his jaw clench as these stories unfolded.

The next evening, her parents sat her down again after the children were tucked into bed. "Your mother and I have been discussing your situation for quite some time. We don't agree with some of the things Kristoffer has done. He's young, and he's made some mistakes. He made us a promise that he would do whatever it took to take care of you. It's not how I would have done things, but I can see that he's keeping his promise. As his wife, your place is at his side, whatever the circumstance. We are so happy to see you and meet our grandchildren, but you were wrong to leave him. You must go home."

Karoline was stunned. She never imagined her parents would take his side. "You're making me leave? You won't support my decision? You don't think your grandchildren deserve better?"

"You will write to him and try to work this out. He will need to send back money for your passage. We can't afford to give it to you. Until then, we will all enjoy your visit," her father said authoritatively. His standing up, like a final piece of punctuation, marked the end of the conversation.

Karoline had been raised to obey, not to argue, so she said nothing else and nodded her assent. She had already said as much as she dared. While she would eventually obey, she would do it in her own time. She was not going back until she had what she wanted. Her father, she noticed, had not given her a time limit. She wondered whether he had forgotten that part, but knowing how detailed he was, she thought he might be trying to do his duty in directing her to return while also siding with her by leaving the timing in her hands. He could save their reputation, especially hers and Kristoffer's, by explaining that she had come for a long visit.

The next afternoon, Karoline set out to visit Runa. Her mother told her Runa had not yet married, and she was working on a farm a few miles from their home. Karoline found Runa in the barn, milking cows. When Runa looked up to see who had entered, she was utterly surprised and joyful.

"Karoline! What are you doing here?"

"I've come home for a while. I just arrived yesterday and wanted to see you as soon as I could."

"Is Kristoffer with you?" she asked while looking around the barn.

"No. I came with only my two babies."

"Two? Turn over a bucket and sit down while I finish the milking."

Karoline found a comfortable position on the overturned milk bucket while Runa sat down on the milking stool and put her head against the cow's warm side. The two women talked through the end of her chores then moved their conversation to Runa's room. Karoline once again relayed her anger and disappointment to a sympathetic ear. She ended her story with her father's decision to make her leave.

"I'm not surprised," Runa said. "He's pretty religious and would expect you to keep your vows. Me? I would have left, too. I think you did the right thing. I'm disappointed you won't be moving back."

Runa had not had an easy time herself since Karoline's leaving. She had lost her position as a nanny due to the children growing too old to need one. It was difficult to find another position, so she had taken a job as a farmhand. She fed chickens, milked cows twice a day, tended the garden, washed laundry, cleaned house, and harvested in the fall. Her hands had become hard and rough, and her skin showed signs of sun and wind damage.

"Did you know that Valter Olsen still isn't married?"

"We don't get any letters from Kristoffer's family, so I have heard nothing about them. How are they doing?"

"Not well. The adult boys have all moved away and found logging and farming jobs. The girls who are old enough to work have been farmed out. I've heard that the oldest girl works mostly in the fields. Valter still lives with his parents, but they aren't able to pay the bank notes. They have more debt on their farm than they can handle. Everyone knows their situation and expects them to lose the farm within the next year. I don't know what will happen to the parents, but Valter will probably go to America. Maybe your brother-in-law will come and live with you?"

Karoline chuckled thinking about Valter in the dugout. "He can have it," she said. "I hope he likes living like a mole."

"How is married life?"

"Not exactly what I thought it would be. Kristoffer was so intimate and fun-loving while we were courting. Once we married, he became bossy and terse. He is certainly not the man I courted."

Karoline told Runa her story. While it still hurt, it seemed that each time she related those awful days, the burden of the story became a little lighter. Runa, the perfect friend, became indignant and angry for her. She displayed the kind of reactions that Karoline had expected from her parents.

The two women said their goodbyes and promised that they would see as much of each other as possible. Runa wanted to see the children, and Karoline felt young again, confiding her feelings to her childhood friend.

Karoline waited several days before she attempted a letter to Kristoffer. She couldn't tell him she was sorry because she wasn't. Even though her parents commanded her to return, she was not sure that she would. Karoline wanted him to understand how afraid she was for their children's lives. Kristoffer had not been there when Inger was dying. Maybe if he had, he would have felt differently about the immediate need to move to a better house. His mind was on the future farm, and he was willing to make sacrifices to get his land. For her, there were limits to those sacrifices. Perhaps his job was to do whatever was necessary to bring about their future, as her father said, but as a mother, her job was to protect her children. She was willing to make her own sacrifices even if that meant sacrificing him.

While she waited for a return letter, she traveled to the Olsens' farm to visit her parents-in-law. She noticed that the farm looked shabbier than the last time she had seen it. She remembered Runa's information about their finances, and now she could see how strapped they were. The house needed paint, and the front porch was starting to sag. The barn looked sad with faded paint and missing shingles. When she knocked on the door, her mother-in-law answered and embraced her warmly. In the parlor sat her father-in-law, also named Kristoffer. As soon as he saw her, he gave her a scowl, put on his boots, and walked out the door. She had wondered how long it would take for the news of her arrival to reach the rest of the community. Obviously, her tale of a long visit had not fooled her in-laws. Her mother-in-law invited her to the kitchen for coffee and cake.

"Karoline, it's so good to see you. I'm sorry about the way Kris treated you. He's angry that you left our son. I told him I was sure you are only home for a visit and that you'll return. Am I right? Tell me how Kristoffer is doing."

Karoline, avoiding her first question said, "He's fine. Things are difficult right now. I just needed to come home and see my family again." Karoline thought it was best to keep the details of their marriage to herself. She didn't know how his family would respond, whether they would take his side. She had a good idea of how his father would feel about her leaving Kristoffer.

"I'm sorry that things are not going well. I had hoped that Kristoffer would be different from his father. I know too well what it is like for you. I've tried to raise my sons to be thoughtful and respectful of women. Unfortunately, so far, that hasn't been the case. Let's talk of other, more pleasant things while you are here. Tell me about my grandchildren."

Karoline politely answered her questions about the children and Minnesota while she watched the woman cuddle her grandchildren. When Karoline inquired about the whereabouts of the rest of the Olsen children, she was informed that most of them were labored out to other families, and those too young were in school.

Karoline did not stay long even though her mother-in-law did well to avoid any more personal questions and tried to connect with her through other women's topics. The tension in the house because of her visit was more than she could withstand. She knew the senior Kristoffer was outside and would stay there until she left his farm.

Karoline visited two more times during her stay, and every time—no matter the time of day—Kristoffer's father would walk out of the house, refusing to acknowledge her or even to look at her. She began to understand the kind of life Kristoffer may have lived with this man as his father.

5 October 1885

Dear Husband,

Ingrid and I arrived safely in Norway on 1 October. My pregnancy ended early once again. I birthed our son on the passage ship and named him Tingvald Atlantic. He is a healthy boy, and I had much help from the other female passengers during my labor. We are all doing well and are at my parents' house.

If you have not looked in your moneybox, then I must confess to you that I took money from it to buy train tickets, but only to Chicago. My sister and her husband generously paid for our expenses to New York City and then to Norway. We are not obliged to repay them because her husband makes a very good living. She said that the money was a gift.

I am not sure when or if I will return. You were not there when our beautiful baby girl struggled to breathe. You did not stay awake at night listening to her lungs. You did not discover her cold, lifeless, fragile body when you woke the next morning. I cannot lose another child because of that dugout. I cannot sacrifice a child made from my own body because you wish to save for the future. What future will there be if our children die?

Our son needs a healthy environment to grow strong. If I bring him back to that miserable damp cave, I will be responsible for his death.

I will consider returning when you have rented us a decent house—one with wooden floors, windows, and plaster walls. When you have secured that for us, please send me the money for our travels.

Sincerely,

Your Wife

12 December 1885

Dear Wife,

Thank you for your correspondence. I can sleep easier now that I know you are well and safe. Please send my greetings to your parents and other family members.

I cannot express how proud I am to receive news of a son. I am anxious to know his features. Does he look more like you or more like me? What color are his hair and eyes? I would have wanted to name him for my own father of whom I carry the same name. Tingvald Atlantic is an odd name.

When you return and we christen him, we will need to give him a different name.

After Inger's funeral, I heard your demand to move. I am not immune to the pain from our daughter's death. I too wept for her. I too felt pain. But it is my duty to build a better life for us. And, I take that responsibility seriously. It is my duty as the man to make the decisions for our family. As the wife, you do not make the decisions.

We cannot go back and undo what has happened to us. We can only move forward. We both knew that coming to America would be difficult, and we knew that our dreams would take hard work. I want my wife and my family by my side. Therefore, you must come back home.

I promise that I will have the money to buy the farm within the next two to three years. If we move to a wood house, it will add another year or more. I am tired of logging, which takes me away from my family. I wish to be my own boss and see my children grow up the way we grew up.

As my wife, it is your duty to obey me. I look forward to your next letter. Include the date of your arrival.

Sincerely,

Your Husband

7 April 1886

Dear Husband,

I received your letter. The children and I are doing well. Ingrid talks constantly, her favorite word being Farfar. She adores my father and follows him throughout the house. She has gone sledding with him several times and loves the snow. Tingvald is a fat baby who smiles and giggles often. He has your wavy hair, but it is auburn like mine. He has your bright blue eyes and high cheekbones. It's difficult to see them under his baby fat. He is small in size like Inger was. I don't think he's going to have his father's height. Between his grandmother and me, he never cries more than a second before one of us has scooped him up and wiped his tears. I'm afraid he is being spoiled.

We went to a church dance last weekend. It reminded me so much of the time we danced together. Your brother Albert, along with a couple of the neighbor men, made sure that I didn't sit along the wall for the entire night. Each of them kindly took me around the dance floor a time or two. I had forgotten how much I enjoy dancing. Though they weren't as good a dancer as you. Stefan Andersen (you may remember him as the young boy on the farm next to us) stepped on my toes when we waltzed. While he is no longer the young boy but now a young, handsome man, he needs to practice more.

How I wished that we could go back in time and dance together again. We could forget the pain of our loss and our now estrangement. But we cannot. As you said in your letter, we can only move forward. For me to move forward, I need to be honest about my feelings. In your letter, you used the word obey—I was to obey you. Children are to obey. Horses are to obey. I am neither of these. As your wife, I am your partner. We will make decisions together, and we will do what is best for our children. If this is not the marriage for you, then I am afraid that I cannot come home again. I want our children to be raised by both of us. I am asking for this one thing: when you have secured a new house for us, then will I return.

Sincerely,

Your Wife

20 August 1886

Dear Karoline,

I am deeply sorry for the words in my last letter. I did not mean to use the word obey in the way that you thought I did. I meant it as a reminder of our wedding vows. Of course you are my partner, but in money matters I know better. As your husband and the children's father, it is my duty to provide for you. This was my promise on our wedding day as well as the promise that I made to your parents. I know that my plans are the best way.

Sacrifice is the best way to achieve those plans. I, too, have made sacrifices. I work from sunup to sundown seven days a week. My work is dangerous, many men having lost their lives in these woods. I cannot come home to my family every evening. I cannot hold my wife and babes. I cannot be the father that I wish to be.

It broke my heart to hear how much time Ingrid spends with her farfar instead of her fadir. I would like to take her sledding myself. I even know which hill we could go down. I want to teach my son how to fish and shoot a gun someday. I want to continue to grow our family.

My plans of owning a farm are closer every day. I stored our belongings in a barn. I am no longer paying rent on the dugout. I stay up at the logging camp and work as many hours as they will give me. My savings have grown, and I have a new plan on how to buy a farm sooner.

Iowa has cheaper land for sale. The Svensen brothers and I are going to purchase it together. We have found a suitable spot in western Iowa. There is a township with many other Norwegian people. I will write to you when we have secured our new farm.

I love you and miss you terribly. I miss our children. Please give each of them many hugs and kisses from their fadir. Give my regards to your parents.

With love,

Kristoffer

15 December 1886

Dearest Karoline,

I hope you and our children are well. I miss you and think of you often. I imagine what our children are doing and what they now look like. I am looking forward to holding them again.

I am proud to tell you that we now own farmland. Our farm is seven miles northeast of a town called Soldier. It is in Willow Township. The soil is as black as night and loamy and rich. It will grow excellent crops. We and the Svensens own thirty acres of tillable land. For now, we will farm it together with the agreement that each will take ten acres when it is time to go our own ways. The land is still sod, so it will take much work to break it up into fine soil.

Our land also has hills and groves of trees. Ravines cut through the pastures where we will one day have cattle. A water source is some distance from where the house will be, but we will dig a well within a year or two. This new land of ours is very different from Norway but very beautiful.

There is no house on the land, but we are going to build you a fine one. It will be small at first, but I will add onto it as our family grows. I promise that it will have windows, and I will build it so that the kitchen faces south. I will put a window over the sink, so you can have sunshine on your face and look out at our beautiful farm. You will have a wood floor to scrub, making it as clean as you please. Ingrid and our son will have their own bedroom. The house will have clean air and light. I promise you this.

I am moving to our new land in one week. The winters in Iowa are milder, so we should be able to start building the house right away. We have found lodging in Soldier and will go every day to work on the house.

For now, it is better that you stay with your parents. You will come home in the spring when the house is finished. I am looking forward to seeing your beautiful face again.

With love,

Kristoffer

30 January 1887

My Dearest Kristoffer,

I received your letter and was so excited to share it with your children and my family. The house sounds like a castle, and the land will yield us a way to live and thrive.

You have done so well. I am so proud to call you my husband.

Ingrid has asked if her room will have a window, too. She also wants to know if there is a sledding hill. She thinks of new house questions every day. She misses her fadir and is looking forward to seeing you again.

Tingvald grows each day. I think he grows out more than he grows up. Except for his coloring, he looks so much like you. He has your face shape and your ears. He is also quick to laugh, like you, and loves playing games. He took a tumble from the sled last week and came up smiling. You would have been proud to see how tough he is.

I am also well. My mother and I complete housework, and I have taken in mending. I want to contribute to our household and am looking forward to our reunion. The house sounds wonderful, and I have started to think about where our meager belongings will go. Please make sure that you build me a big pantry. I am already planning a large garden and will put up vegetables to sustain us through the winters.

There is a ship to America in early April. The children and I will be on it. We should be in western Iowa by the end of the month. Please send the necessary money to bring your wife and children home to you.

All my love,

Karoline

1905

Overheated and tired, but mostly stressed, Karoline finally reached Ames. Because she was unfamiliar with central Iowa, she had not realized that the town was located south of her path. When she reached Pilot Mound, she had asked a farmer hauling watermelons to give her directions. When he pointed behind her, she had nearly started to cry. She would have to turn south and make a diagonal line back through Fraser, Boone, and eventually Ames. Her error had cost her two days.

She imagined what the ice blocks must look like and even further dared to imagine what Kristoffer's body must look like. The clean, even level of bright yellow straw would now be soggy and conforming to the ice and body. They had not put his body into a coffin because her son-in-law was making a beautiful one back home. They had only wrapped him in a tarp, the same kind that covered the wagon. The ice blocks had been packed around and over him. If there wasn't enough ice packed around the body now, it would have started to deteriorate, turning black. Turkey vultures began to circle overhead two days ago. Karoline wasn't interested in taking off the wagon's tarp until absolutely necessary, and she would never take off the body's tarp, wishing to remember him as he was on the day he had walked away from her.

She had finally reached Ames and felt herself relax. She would no longer worry day and night about the ice. Ames was roughly halfway to Soldier, so a new supply should last her, but her first task was to find the icehouse.

Karoline eventually came to Hoggatt Street and stopped at the first business, a druggist's store, to ask for directions. She was nervous about asking because her English was so crude. Having lived among her own people her whole life, she had never become fluent in the language. Her children learned English when they went to school and tried to teach her the basics. Otherwise, they spoke and interpreted for their parents when the need arose. This trip was the first time she had to speak and interpret for herself.

When she entered the store, she saw a short, bald man with a round face. He wore small spectacles on his chubby red nose. "Please, sir, where icehouse?"

"Icehouse? This town don't have an icehouse. All of our ice comes from Des Moines. They got a huge icehouse there on the Des Moines River. They ship it up to us by rail. How much you needin'?"

Stunned, Karoline stood there looking at the druggist, tears sliding down her cheeks. She had missed much of what he said, but she did understand that Ames did not have an icehouse. She also caught the words *Des Moines*, which she had heard when she left several days ago.

"Ma'am, please, come round here and have a seat. Let me get you somethin' to drink." He gestured her to the stool behind his display case. Karoline went around the counter and sat on a short stool. Her mind was a rainfall of questions: Would she have to go to Des Moines? How far was Des Moines? Should she try to make it home without it? Should she try to buy some ice from local vendors? Should she stay a few days and see if she could buy it from the train station?

"Here you go, Ma'am. Just take it easy and rest yourself."

He had brought her a cold Coca-Cola. As she looked down into the glass, she could see the shaved ice floating on the top. She began to cry again. Through her sobbing, she told this kind man her problem.

"I don't know what to do. My wagon is on street and is the body of my husband. I come from Cedar Falls. Many days. Ice no more. I need ice. Cedar Falls man say ice here."

Vernon Gibbs, the proprietor, didn't understand. Karoline gestured him out to her wagon. She pointed to the back of her wagon and said, "Husband." She didn't know the word for died because she had never had the need for it, so she closed her eyes and crossed her hands over her chest as she had seen at funerals. She then pointed to the water pooling below her wagon and said, "Need ice."

"Oh, my dear Lord, ma'am. You're in quite a fix. I'd give ya what I got, but I can't go without my ice until another batch arrives. Now, we can think of somethin'. Just let me see if I can put my head together with a couple of the other merchants and come up with a solution. You just rest here, and I'll be back."

He promptly stood up, turned over his "Open" sign, and walked out the door. Karoline hadn't understood everything he said, but she caught enough to understand his intentions. Within a few minutes, he was back with two other men. After many ideas were formed and thrown away, they came up with what they thought was the best one: they settled on the college.

Iowa State College of Agriculture and Mechanic Arts was a

rapidly growing institution just north of Ames. They had added a veterinary program, which worked with dead animals. Requiring a great
deal of ice to preserve the animals for the students' use, the college
was sure to have large amounts of it, the men reasoned. They also
probably bought more than they needed. Because they also used the
ice for other facility operations, they may even have received a load
of ice every two to three days. Perhaps they would be willing to spare
some for this emergency.

The men put signs on their establishments to indicate a long
lunch break and took Karoline up to the college, the druggist riding
in her wagon with her. As they traveled, Karoline told the druggist,
Vernon Gibbs, her entire story as best as she could. He was a kind
man who reciprocated with sympathy and troubles of his own. Even
though they didn't understand everything the other said, Karoline
appreciated the conversation. She hadn't realized how deprived of
human interaction she had been these many days. More so, she
missed having someone with whom she could share her problems
and not be left to solve them alone. Vernon had reassured her several
times that they would figure this out and get her some ice.

The rest of the afternoon was spent going from one college building to the next, looking for someone who could help them. Eventually, they made their way to the veterinary building. The custodian
of veterinary supplies, who had lost his own wife two years before,
felt deep empathy for Karoline's situation and agreed to sell her the
ice she needed at cost.

The custodian, along with Vernon and the other business propri-
etors, took it upon themselves to reload the ice. When they pulled
back the wagon's tarp, Karoline could see them flinch from the smell.
They quickly repacked the ice and spread a fresh layer of straw
across it. They did not unwrap Kristoffer's body. She had chosen to
stand farther off, avoiding any curiosity to look into the wagon.

Given their reaction to its smell, she speculated that the body had started to rot.

By the time they had finished, the sun was starting to descend, announcing the supper hour. Vernon invited her to go back to his house and stay the evening with him, his wife Margie, and their four children. Normally, Karoline would have declined given her shyness, poor language skills, and dislike for charity; but both her body and her soul were exhausted, allowing her to accept someone else taking care of her. "Thank you," she said in response.

1887

Kristoffer met Karoline and the children at the train station in Denison, a small town southeast of Soldier.

Stepping down from the train, she felt her heart jump when she caught sight of him. His hair and beard were longer, and he looked like a man who had no woman to take care of him. Back in Norway, Karoline had convinced herself she no longer loved him, but feeling her heart start the moment she saw him told her otherwise.

Kristoffer reached out for his son right away and held him while looking into his face. "Hello, little one. I'm your *fadir*." He handed Tingvald back to Karoline and went to scoop up Ingrid, but she hid behind her mother's skirts. Karoline knew she did not remember him, and she could see the hurt in Kristoffer's eyes. He then turned his attention to Karoline. He hugged her and kissed her on the cheek. Karoline could not read his face and did not know whether he had forgiven her for running away, but his embrace felt good.

From Denison, it would be another three or four hours to Soldier. As they traveled by wagon, they crossed rolling hills and flatlands. It was beautiful country with plenty of green trees and grass. There were no bodies of water, just the rippling of prairie grass. The land closer to Denison was already being planted with corn, beans, and milo; but the fields turned to wild prairie the farther northwest they rode.

Once they were travelling on the open road, Kristoffer asked, "How are your parents getting along?"

"They are well. Everything seems to be the same with them."

"And the town? Is there any news since we've been away?"

"Not very much. Everything looked the same."

"Did you see my family? Are they well?"

"I stopped by with the children a few times. They enjoyed meeting their grandchildren. Your family are all healthy. Your mother sends her love. It's a beautiful day today, don't you think?" Karoline wanted to avoid talking about her time in Norway because she was afraid that it would bring up unwanted discussion.

"*Ja*. It's a good day for planting."

This man felt like a stranger to her. Their conversation remained stilted, and she thought they were walking farther away from the very thing they should have been discussing. Neither wanted to upset the other, and she suspected that perhaps Kristoffer was trying to keep himself from letting her see his anger and disappointment. Instead of facing the topic head-on, Karoline decided to keep this peaceful conversation and enjoy the ride to her new home.

After several hours, Kristoffer raised his hand and pointed out their farm to her. She observed steep hills with newly-planted corn and pastures with groves of trees and deep ravines from once-running water.

Their house sat on a hill with a grove of trees behind it. The small

house next to those large oaks reminded her of a child next to a group
of grown-ups. She hadn't known what to expect of the house, but it
was much smaller than she had anticipated. Her new home consisted
of two small bedrooms and a kitchen joined to a main room. Kristoffer could see the disappointment on her face and quickly told her of
his plans to expand each fall after the harvest. Before they entered
the house, he took her to the south side, which was the kitchen wall.
He had built a dumb waiter on the outside of the house. It was the
size of a packing crate with shelves inside. He showed her how it
lowered into the deep, cylindrical hole in the ground. There, they
could keep cold their dairy and meats. She was proud of his ingenu-
ity and concern for her convenience. He also pointed out the window
so that she could look out while she was in the kitchen. She knew
that he was pointing out more than the window: he had kept his
promise.

When she walked into her house, she saw two grown men sitting
in rocking chairs with their stocking feet up on her side table. They
were both in their mid-twenties with blonde hair and blonde-red
beards. They looked rather imposing with their tall frames and mus-
cular builds, but their voices were soft and gentle. Upon seeing her,
they both jumped up to greet her.

"Karoline, this is Elfred and Olof Svensen. They live here with
us."

Her lungs expelled all of her breath, and she couldn't quite grasp
exactly what Kristoffer was telling her. How could they live with
them? There were only two bedrooms. Where did they sleep? And
for how long would they stay?

Elfred and Olof shook her hand and asked about her trip home.
They turned their attention to her children, and she could see that
they were naturally paternal. Whether their actions had been purposeful she didn't know, but they had done the exact right thing in

being interested in her children.

Once in her own bed that night, she hashed it out with Kristoffer. "Why are they living in our house? Are our children to always sleep in the main room on the floor? What about winter?"

Kristoffer turned to her in the dark and said, "Karoline, I'm sorry. I know this isn't what you expected, but I had no choice. In order to get the house done as it is, I needed their help. They built us a house so that you would come home, which meant they had no house of their own. And I wouldn't have gotten this far on the building without them. Was I supposed to tell them that they couldn't live here because it was ours? Would you have me throw them out with no place to go? We all farm together. I can't clear this hard sod without their help. They will stay until we can get their house built, but that means no adding on to this house before then. Give them a chance. I think you'll grow to appreciate them."

As much as she wanted to argue back, she couldn't. He was right this time. They would have to make do.

The next morning, she woke up early to prepare breakfast in her own kitchen. When the Svensens came to the table, she was shy around them. She had never been good with conversing, especially with men, and two of them at the same time left her tongue without words. The brothers, however, were jovial and loved to laugh. They showed interest in her past and asked her many questions about her family's farm. Eventually, she could feel herself loosening up, wanting to know more about them.

Elfred and Olof Svensen were two years apart. Their father died when they were ten and twelve, leaving their mother to raise eight children on her own. Unfortunately, she couldn't afford to keep all of her children, and the two oldest boys, Elfred and Olof, were sent to their relatives. They lived with their father's brother and worked the farm with him and his sons, but they never really felt part of the family. When they were old enough, they left their uncle's home and got jobs in the logging industry. Elfred was sixteen, and Olof was fourteen. When they had saved enough money, like many other Norwegian men, they bought passage to America. Their story was the same as her and Kristoffer's at that point. They had landed in St. Paul because of the logging jobs. They had been living in the logging tents for eight years. The loggers were their family. Two years before the Olsens' arrival, they had finally rented a house close to St. Paul. They had hoped to find a pair of wives to live with them. However, they spent most of their time in the camps and had done little socializing with women. When Kristoffer shared that his wife had gone back to Norway, they jumped to help him. They were both ready for something different and wanted a permanent home. They were still close to their mother and sent money to her to help raise the rest of the children.

Each day, while the men left to work the fields, she cleaned her house and organized it. She scrubbed the wood floor and washed the windows inside and outside. She made curtains for all the windows, and she took her mending money and bought a few things they needed: blankets, dishes, washtubs, and material for the children's clothes. Although the house was plain and tiny, she felt proud of it. She worked hard to make it as pleasant as she could.

Having the Svensens live with them had been an adjustment at first. However, the brothers were polite, and she could tell that they had been raised well. When they came home in the evening, they washed outside, took off their shoes, thanked her profusely for their food, and always called her "ma'am." Elfred and Olof also did what they could—watched the children while she cooked, helped hang laundry on the line, brought up water from the spring, and built the fire in the stove each morning—to make themselves more helpful to her.

In the evenings, the four adults sat in front of the fireplace and sang along with Elfred's guitar. He was an excellent player and knew a catalog of Scandinavian songs. Both men had beautiful voices and brought warmth to their home while they sang. She grew to think of these two men as part of their family. They worried about her, smothered the children with love, and made Kristoffer laugh and joke once again.

One morning, after she returned from church, the Svensens surprised her with a freshly tilled garden. They explained that their mother's garden was everything to her: a way to feed her family, a way to get away from her family, and a way to soothe her worries. They hoped that Karoline would feel about her garden the way their mother felt about hers.

Karoline was excited to have her first garden. Unlike women who had been expanding their gardens with replanted seeds, Karoline's first patch was small. Had she been in the house last winter, she would have ordered her seeds from a catalogue. Each harvest, she would have kept the seeds from her produce to plant the next spring. This first year, though, she would plant what she could get from other women. Because the brothers had such vibrant and friendly personalities, they had made connections with families in Soldier and introduced her to women in the community who then were generous in giving her starts from their plants. In spite of their being ripped from their home, the scraggly starts acclimated well to the new soil and eventually started to grow. Karoline watched over them like they were her own children. Her first harvest brought meager produce, and the family ate all of it with nothing left to put up. Karoline was proud to be able to contribute to their family's needs, making plans to add more kinds of produce and more of everything the following spring.

Within a month of her return, she was pregnant for the third time. Her pregnancy went well, and she felt healthy while her body grew larger. She was tired by midafternoon, which made the men of the house more helpful. Elfred and Olof pampered her by doing additional chores, and Kristoffer bought her a milk cow so that she and the children could get fresh milk daily. Kristoffer seemed to be a different man while expecting this third child: he prepared better this time and found a midwife for her several months before she was due. The baby was expected in February, which made Karoline worry about snowstorms. She remembered her traumatic first time with the twins and dreamed often that she was completely alone to deliver this child. The men promised her that she would not be alone. Kristoffer would stay with her while the brothers fetched the midwife.

True to their word, they brought the midwife to her when she went into labor. All three men stayed in the sitting room, the brothers keeping the children occupied while Kristoffer added wood to the stove and fireplace and completed other odd jobs to keep busy. Within a few hours, she had delivered a healthy baby girl. They named her Elizabeth Marie, calling her Betsi.

When the weather grew warmer, they christened both her and Tingvald at the Lutheran church in Soldier. Kristoffer had not brought up Tingvald's name change again. The toddler had learned his name, and Kristoffer decided to leave well enough alone since they finally had peace in the house.

1905

Karoline left her new friends, the Gibbs family, early the next morning. She felt renewed by her stay. Margie Gibbs had fed her a large meal, heated water for a proper bath, and put her in a bedroom away from the children's noise. She slept like the dead and dreamed of her first year in the new house. They were pleasant dreams that brought back the Svensen brothers, one of whom had died in recent years. Olof Svensen had caught smallpox the same year as her Ole.

Ten months after Betsi's birth, Karoline had Kristian Aleksander, calling him Alex. And a year later in October, twins Gunda and Sofie joined their family.

Her large group of children began to make the house feel as though it would burst at the seams. After Betsi was born, the men added two additional bedrooms to the house, but there was still little room for anyone to find peace and certainly no room where one could sit and think. With six children, the oldest being five, the house filled with babies crying, dirty clouts soaking, and years of endless night feedings. Karoline rose with the sun and began her daily tasks—breakfast making, breakfast cleaning, laundry washing and hanging, lunch making, lunch cleaning, gardening, supper making, supper cleaning, and needlework by candlelight—only to fall into bed at night and start again the next morning. Often the daily chores were done with an ever-growing perpetually pregnant belly.

After three and a half years with them, the Svensen brothers decided to move to Soldier. The crops had done very well the first year, giving them enough money to purchase a house for themselves after they sold off ten of their acres to Kristoffer. They decided that farming was less stable than logging, and because they were such social men, they enjoyed being around more people. They opened their own feed and seed store. The farmers had been going to Denison to buy their supplies, so they were more than pleased to keep their business in town. As a result, the Svensens' store did very well.

When the brothers left, the house seemed strange. A large invisible hole had opened up in Karoline's days. She missed their constant concern about her feelings and her welfare. She missed their chatter at the breakfast table. She missed the sound of her children uproariously laughing, knowing that one of the men had caused it. They had treated her the way she had always wanted from Kristoffer. She often thought about her time in the dugout. She was fairly certain that neither one of those men would have allowed her to live in it. They would never have stayed there after a child of theirs had died. She did not love either of the men, but the way they looked after her and worried about her was the kind of relationship she thought she would have with a spouse. Even though by then they had espoused themselves as stolid bachelors, she felt that they would make very good husbands to a pair of lucky sisters.

Within a few months of their absence, Kristoffer reverted back to his former self: he was less solicitous and spent time in the barn after he'd finished his supper instead of coming into the house to keep her company. He talked less at the table and was irritated more quickly when the children cried. The farm naturally demanded most of his attention and kept him outside, creating a rift between them. She wasn't sure what she had perhaps done to create the further divide.

Kristoffer was a stoic man. He did not profess his love to her, nor did he express any kind of anger. He was very different with the children, however. He kissed and hugged each one of them every time he came in from the fields. If they fell and hurt themselves, he was tender with them, holding them on his lap and stroking their hair.

Karoline had come to understand that he would never forgive her for leaving him. She had disobeyed and embarrassed him. The men at the logging camp as well as his family knew that she had taken money from him and had gone back to her family for a year and a half. Even to the last day, when she watched him walk away from her, she knew that he still held her disloyalty against her. It had faded some over the years, but he never trusted her completely again.

His lack of trust was probably why she had assigned herself the last wifely duty of bringing him home. She could have sent his body on the train, but she had pictured him in cargo, among passengers' baggage or perhaps with shipping crates full of goods for the merchants. It seemed impersonal and almost cruel to treat him that way. Her sense of duty for her life mate outweighed her own anger and disappointment. She had insisted to her sons that she go alone to bring him home. She knew she was trying to atone for her failings. Karoline hoped that he could see her dedication to him and would finally forgive her, if only from the other side.

1891

Karoline had been busy with the mountain of laundry all morning and didn't realize the lunch hour had passed until she looked up and saw that it was already one-thirty. She had fed the children at noon so that they wouldn't be hungry while waiting for their father to come in for lunch. Since she was experiencing the signs of morning sickness, she wasn't in the mood to eat. What puzzled her was how late Kristoffer was.

Kristoffer had been plowing the ten acres nearest the house. Every day around noon, he returned to the farm to water the horse and eat his lunch. Sometimes he walked through the door exactly at noon; other times, he may arrive closer to one o'clock. But he was never later than that.

She began to think of the possible reasons he had not returned home. If a horse had gone lame, he would have brought it back to the barn immediately. If the plow had broken one of its tines, he would have had to come home and retrieve supplies to mend it. He would have stopped by the house to tell her and possibly take his lunch with him. A more likely reason would be their new horse. Kristoffer had purchased a partially broken horse at the animal auction in Dunlap. Half-broken horses were certainly cheaper but definitely caused more problems for those who gambled on them. He had named her Millie, and she was a black beauty with a white forehead and fetlocks. Kristoffer assured her that Millie would settle down once she was hooked to the wagon with Charlie, their old horse. Charlie was no longer good for farm work, but he was a gentle horse for the children to ride and would calm Millie when they pulled together.

Millie took off on a dead run a week ago. Kristoffer had had to chase her a quarter of a mile before she slowed down. Karoline was sure that it had happened again. He was probably out chasing her down at that very minute.

With the laundry hung up, Karoline turned her attention to her garden. They had experienced a mild spring, which gave her an opportunity to get the planting done early. Her lettuce thrived, and she picked some every day. It was so nice to have fresh greens again for supper. She also pulled a few radishes. She liked to eat them while they were smaller, so they weren't so hot. Once she was done with the picking, she started her weeding. It seemed that the weeds were the fastest growing vegetation. Each day she cleaned up her rows, and the very next day new plants sprang up. Her strawberries were in particular need.

She had ordered the strawberries from a seed catalog two years ago, and now she had a thick but small patch. Last year, there weren't many berries, but she had expected that. With each year, her patch would produce more of those sweet red gems. Eventually, she would have enough to make strawberry jams and pies. Now, she could only hope for enough strawberries to top a cake—and that was after the children had surreptitiously picked a few each day.

She had expected Kristoffer to show up by the time she returned to the house. He was not one to skip a meal. He got light headed if he didn't eat. Nearing three thirty, the lateness of the day started to worry her. This had to be about more than a runaway horse. A feeling in the pit of her stomach told her it was something serious.

Karoline stepped outside her door and peered across the land. She did not see Kristoffer, but she wasn't surprised because she could only see a short distance due to the hills.

She needed to decide on her next actions. Always one to get additional help, Karoline thought about walking the six miles to town and getting one of the Svensen brothers. Traveling that distance would take her two hours. By the time she got there, it would be five thirty. If he was hurt, that could mean the difference between life and death.

Her other option was to find him herself. She could saddle Charlie and look for him, but if he was hurt, she would need the wagon. Karoline's greatest concern was getting him into it. If he was unconscious or couldn't stand, she wouldn't be able to lift him. She would have to get another man to help her.

Either way, she would need to leave the children in the care of Ingrid, who was now seven years old. If she was only gone a few hours, Ingrid could manage. If she was gone any longer, she would have two things to worry her.

Karoline decided to find him. She retrieved Charlie from the barn and put the collar on him. He knew well what was next and went to the wagon on his own. She backed him into the wagon and hooked him up. Karoline was glad that she had been made to hook up a horse since she was a teenager. Her father had said that if she was going to drive the wagon, she needed to know how to do everything that it involved. He had taken her out several days and made her hook up their horse, correcting her mistakes and making her start over. She'd been angry with him for making her practice so many times. A few times, she'd even thrown the collar to the ground and stomped into the house, but her father had always come in after her and made her finish what she started. Today, she understood his reasoning and thanked him.

Once Charlie was harnessed and Ingrid was settled, she set out east into the field. In the far corner, she saw the unhooked plow, turned over, but no horse and no husband. Obvious drag marks were in the black soil, and she followed them in her wagon. They continued east and eventually stopped when they came to a grove of trees.

The old oak grove was where Kristoffer and the Svensens had stopped clearing the land. The grass and weeds grew tall between the tightly packed trees. Underneath were layers of dead leaves and weeds. Some of the trees had large broken limbs, which lay beneath their canopy, their bark shedding like skin. Other trees had been cut down and used for her house. Their stumps, though, were still nearly as tall as she. Karoline had warned the children never to go into the grove because of snakes. The tall grass made a perfect home for them. She wasn't sure what kind of snakes lived in Iowa and whether they were venomous or not, but her own fear of them made her pass along her phobia.

Karoline had no choice but to enter the grove. She grabbed the bottom hem of the back of her dress and threaded it between her legs, tucking it into her belt, fashioning herself a ridiculous looking pair of pants, but she would rather have looked ridiculous than have her dress drag along the weeds, picking up burrs and other refuse. She filled her lungs and let out the air slowly, gaining her courage. She put one foot solidly onto the ground, listening for any animal movement. Step by step, she started to cover the grove, yelling Kristoffer's name.

About a quarter mile into the grove, she saw his handkerchief on the ground. Excited to finally find some evidence, she began looking in a circular pattern. Eventually, she saw his red shirt among the brush. Karoline rushed over to him, calling his name, but he did not respond or move. His clothes were filthy from being dragged, and he had a gash on his head, leaking bright red blood. Other than that, he didn't seem to be hurt anywhere else. He must have hit his head, giving him a concussion, because she could see him breathing. She shook him and patted his face. Nothing. She sat him up and pounded on his back. Eventually, he woke up. He was groggy and said his head hurt. When he tried to move, he felt a sharp pain in his side, indicating he had probably cracked some ribs. Karoline put his arm around her shoulders, but she was too small and he was too heavy to get him up. She then found a thick bough, and they used that so he could boost himself up. When he stepped down onto his right foot, he let out a yelp, which meant that he had broken his ankle, and sat back down.

"I can't walk on my foot. How are you going to get me out of here?"

"The wagon is at the edge of the grove, so you only need to walk to the edge. You can use me to lean on as well as that stick. You'll have to hop."

Karoline got him up on his left foot. Each time she put her arm around his waist while he hopped forward, he let out another scream, and she apologized for hurting him. They went on—hopping and screaming and apologizing—until they reached the wagon. It took them twice as long on the journey out because he had to climb over limbs and rocks.

Karoline got him into the wagon and rode slowly across the uneven field. "How did this happen to you?"

"I had to unhook the plow from Millie. Since I needed both of my hands to fix the plough, I tied her reins to my wrist since she won't stay put. A ground squirrel ran in front of her, spooking her. She took off at a dead run, pulling me along with her. She dragged me across the field and into the grove. I must have hit a dozen rocks in that field. The reins finally broke where I lay. Look, I still have a piece of the them tied to my wrist." He held up his wrist to show her.

They finally reached the house around six. They could hear the children crying from outside of the house. Other than their being hungry, all was well. Ingrid had taken charge and had even changed a clout. Her face was pale and her blue eyes wide from a little fear and a lot of worry, but she had proven that she was old enough to start helping out more.

Karoline got Kristoffer into their bed. His ankle, swelling and turning colors, worried her. If they had been in Norway, she would have put ice on it to keep the swelling down, but on the prairie there was none. She did her best to make him comfortable.

"I need to fetch the doctor. If we don't get your ankle set, you won't walk again. I'm going to make the children a quick supper, and then I'll go to Soldier."

His face pained, Kristoffer nodded his assent. She made a quick supper of scrambled eggs and left Ingrid in charge once more.

Karoline unhitched Charlie and put on the saddle. It was faster to ride him instead of hooking him to the wagon. The doctor would bring his own buggy, so she didn't need to think of anyone other than herself.

The doctor did his best to set the ankle and wrap it tightly, but there was no guarantee that Kristoffer would walk as well again. He then wrapped Kristoffer's ribs, which was all he could do. His last order was for the patient to stay in bed for at least a month. With planting unfinished, someone else was needed to complete the farm work.

The next day, Karoline was out of bed at dawn, getting the children's meals ready for the day. Ingrid was in charge once again, and Tingvald would be going to the field with his mother. As she looked out her kitchen window, she saw Millie eating the tender plants in her garden. The horse still had the collar on and dragged the reins behind her. Karoline went out to the garden, seized her by her halter, and led her into the barn. She would take Charlie to the field instead.

With the reins tied together and around her neck, Karoline placed her hands on the plow handles, putting some weight on them. She clucked her tongue for Charlie and started walking forward, pushing the plow tine into the soil as they went, but the tine barely scratched the surface. She stopped, bore down harder on the handles, and started again—this time digging a deeper groove. It didn't take long for her arms and shoulders to tire, and she was thrown off balance occasionally as she straddled the furrow. The reins dug into her neck, and her hands started to chafe from the handles. The sun punished them both, and clouds of gnats swarmed around her face. She had never been this miserable in her whole life. Tingvald walked behind her, dropping seeds into the groove and covering them with dirt. They worked silently all morning and only made one pass across the field.

As they stood on the other side, looking back at their work, Karoline could see the crookedness of her rows, especially in comparison to Kristoffer's. Her shoulders and arms ached, and she didn't know if she could make it the entire day—not to speak of how tired Tingvald must be with his short legs. While she couldn't imagine how long it was going to take them to finish even one field, she made them continue after eating a short lunch under the trees. The hours dragged on as she became more heated and sore.

After a full day, Karoline and Tingvald walked into the house for supper, which Karoline would need to fix. Her body ached, her hands were raw, her neck was sunburned, and she just wanted to bathe and fall into bed. But there was laundry to soak, and there were children to clean. She was beginning to realize there was no way that she could do field work every day and keep the house running. Ingrid could wash the dishes, sweep the floors, and weed the garden; but she didn't have the upper body strength to scrub and wring out laundry. With two babies still in clouts, it wouldn't be long before they had dirtied them all. She had no idea how she was going to manage, but she would have to figure out something.

Karoline rose at daybreak once again, this time also waking Ingrid and Tingvald. She got the stove going and directed Ingrid in making the eggs. She felt confident Ingrid could feed the children both breakfast and lunch; so she packed up what she and Tingvald needed, hooked up Charlie, and headed back to the field.

Yesterday's work in the field had taught her to dress more thoughtfully. She wore her lightest dress and left her petticoat in the house. She also wore her garden hat with the wide brim and borrowed a pair of Kristoffer's gloves.

By eleven, the heat had risen to ninety degrees. The Iowa humidity made it feel more like one hundred. Her body, soaked with sweat, ached so much that she could only focus on her pain. Her head throbbed from the heat and strain, her arms felt lifeless, and her lower back had a stabbing pain. From behind her, she heard Tingvald say, "Mama, I'm tired. Can we sit down for awhile?"

"No. We need to continue. We have to finish this field." Her voice sounded harsh, and she wished that she could comply with his request.

By mid-afternoon, she could see that she had made less progress than the day before. If this rate continued, how many weeks would it take them to finish all three fields? Finally, she just sat down in the dirt and covered her face with her hands. Karoline just wanted to take her child and walk back to her house. She didn't think she had it in her to continue any further.

"Hello! Karoline!" shouted Olof Svensen from atop his horse. "How are you getting along? I heard about Kristoffer's accident."

"Olof? Hello. Yes, he's laid up in the house with broken ribs and a broken ankle. He's going to be in bed for the next month, at least. Maybe longer. We're not sure when he'll be back in the field. As you can see, I'm doing my best."

"Karoline, stop. Take Tingvald and go back to your house. Leave the farming to us. I've talked to some of the other farmers, and they've volunteered to come on Sundays with their equipment and finish the planting. You don't need to be out here."

Relief flooded through her body. What would she and Kristoffer have done without these two men? Karoline gratefully gathered up Tingvald and headed back to the house.

Kristoffer had gotten out of bed and hobbled to a chair. When she and Tingvald walked in, he showed his surprise. "Are you eating lunch here? Or did something happen to the plow?"

"No. Olof Svensen came out to the field to see me. He has gathered some other farmers to complete the planting. He told me to come home, and he would take care of everything."

Angry, Kristoffer replied, "I don't want help from other farmers. We can do our own planting. I'm going to tell him not to come and certainly not to bring other men. We'll figure this out for ourselves."

"*We* can do the planting, Kristoffer? I'm the only one who can do the plowing in this family, and I'm telling you that I can't do it anymore. My body is not strong enough. I didn't even get done half as much as I did yesterday. And, what about taking care of the children and this house? Ingrid has been trying her best, but she can't keep up. And I am too exhausted when I come home to take on the housework. I know you don't want to take charity, but it's our only option. I'm not going back out into that field and neither are you, so what other choice do we have?"

Kristoffer sat in the chair with no response. She knew he was trying to think of any way around charity. She was sure he was mentally considering their finances to gauge whether he could pay the men, but they couldn't. Finally, he conceded with a "fine" and went back to the bedroom.

Ten farmers, two being the Svensen brothers, came with their horses the following Sunday. Within three Sundays, they had all thirty acres planted. As much as Kristoffer and Karoline hated charity, they learned to accept neighborly concern, knowing that one day they would return the favor.

1905

As Karoline navigated the wagon, she thought about the friends who had helped them when Kristoffer was unable to farm along with the kind people who had helped her so far in her journey. She was appreciative of Iowa folks' kind hearts and concern for their neighbors. As a result, she thought of America as her home even more than she did Norway. In the beginning of her marriage, she had been resentful of being away from her family. It was not until she had planted her roots in Iowa that she had stopped wishing to return to Norway.

Ironically, the one person in her life who should have felt like home had felt more like a stranger. Over the course of their marriage, Karoline had often angrily recognized that there were some friends who would do more for her than her own husband. If those friends had not reached out when Kristoffer had his accident, they might have starved to death. It turned out that Kristoffer had been laid up in the house closer to two months. During those months, Karoline had experienced some of the worst days of her marriage.

The first few days after the accident, she'd been working in the garden, so she didn't have to listen to his complaints. When she was in the house, he slept for long periods of time. By the end of the first week, though, he became more demanding of the family, complaining constantly about things not being done correctly. She and the children became prisoners of his beckoning. When he yelled for something, they were expected to bring it to him within minutes. When he wasn't calling for something, he was yelling about something else: the children were too loud, lunch was late, the chickens needed feeding. Since Kristoffer could do nothing himself, he used his family like an extension. Anything that came into his head that needed doing, he bellowed for one of them to do it. If Karoline went out to the garden to get some peace, he was angry that she did not come when he called.

The children often became scarce after breakfast. They volunteered for the outside chores—milking the cow, feeding the chickens, working in the garden, hanging laundry—just to get away from him. When they did have the misfortune of being berated by him, they often cried, which made Kristoffer even more angry. Karoline then became angry with him for hurting the children, but she could not protect them from his ire.

Karoline tried her best to have patience and not let his criticisms hurt her because she knew he was acting out in frustration for his situation. He was embarrassed to have the other farmers completing his work. He felt unmanly for being unable to provide the work needed to feed his family.

Karoline became concerned about how this time period was impacting the children's relationship with their father. They did not understand why he was being harsh toward them. They became afraid of him and resented the way he spoke to them. Because they were the oldest, Ingrid and Tingvald carried the permanent effects. They were never close to their father again and shied away from him when he tried to hug or kiss them. The younger children didn't remember specifically what he had said to them, but they maintained their distance well into their teenage years. It saddened Karoline to see their relationship with their father so strained. He had been a good father to them, and if he hadn't had the accident, they would have been as close to him as Karoline was to her father.

When Kristoffer finally recovered and complained about the way the children had treated him, she tried to explain the effects of his past treatment. His response to her was the same as it had been when she had asked to move out of the dugout. Since he was the father, they should respect him and treat him as was fitting for his position in the household.

Once again, Kristoffer could not understand the tenderness of the heart. He had been raised with a heavy, distant hand. His own father had neither hugged nor kissed his children. He considered his duty to provide for them to be his only obligation. In the same way, Kristoffer expected respect. Karoline could understand why Kristoffer behaved in this way. He had never seen anything else. His father had established the mold, and Kristoffer didn't know any other way existed, but knowing this about him didn't make it any easier to be with him. He thought he showed his love every time he went out into the field to work from sunup to sundown. He thought he showed his love by taking his sons with him when they were old enough to teach them how to farm. He thought he showed his love to his daughters by being strict with them, so they would grow into respectable women and find good husbands. But what he really showed was a man who didn't know how to love.

And now, as she traveled with his body, was she doing the same?

So far, she hadn't shed even one tear for him. To survive her marriage, had she hardened her heart to withstand his lack of tenderness? Was her heart so calloused with the many abrasions he had given her that she no longer could feel love for him?

When she finally reached Soldier, there would be an outpouring of concern because she had lost her mate. Piles of food made by concerned hands would be waiting for her. Her neighbors would make a special trip to her house to ask her how she was holding up and to offer their help. Their hearts would feel pain for her loss. Her church congregation would weep for her and the children. Karoline was already starting to imagine the funeral: long hugs, kisses, hand-holding. She would have to greet each and every person who came to support her. And she would have to pretend for them.

1891

Karoline knew that if she didn't get out of that house, she would be tempted to put a pillow over Kristoffer's head and suffocate him. He had been laid up for a month, and she had endured his bellowing and complaining and criticizing every day of it. This morning, he criticized Tingvald for ten minutes on the way he had put away the horses. At only seven years old, Tingvald did his very best. However, he was not tall or strong enough to do the same kind of job Kristoffer would have done. Karoline tried to protect him as best she could, but the little boy's self-esteem had suffered a harsh berating, and seeing the tears slide down his cheeks as he stood in their bedroom and listened to Kristoffer scold him for not trying hard enough, left another hole in Karoline's heart.

After she departed the house, she headed south. A good stout walk would settle her anger and give her time to think of how to repair the damage. The sun was warm on her skin, and there was no breeze. The oak trees wore a new set of bright green leaves, the wild magnolias showed off their white blooms and perfumed the air, and the tall, stately elms hosted bright male cardinals that were whistling to attract their mates. She could smell the wet, black soil. Iowa was so beautiful in the spring.

As she came to the top of the hill, she could see the farmhouse half a mile off. The farmland was being rented out, and the house itself had been sitting empty for several years. But today, she saw smoke coming from the chimney. She decided to head over to the house to introduce herself. As she got closer, she noticed laundry hanging on the line and the front door open to let in the early June weather.

Coming into the farmyard, she observed a woman about her age in the garden. The woman, small in stature like herself, had long blonde hair, which had been plaited into a braid and hung down her back.

"Hello," Karoline called out. "I'm Karoline, your neighbor," she said, pointing back toward her house.

The woman looked up. Karoline could see her bright blue eyes and fair complexion. She was a pretty woman with a heart-shaped face and a kind smile.

"Good morning. It's nice to see you. I'm Kristina Jorgensen. My husband Stefan and I just moved into this house. Would you like to come in and have some coffee?"

"That's so kind of you. Yes, I would."

When Karoline stepped into the house, she was pleased to see a tidy kitchen. A vase of purple and gold wildflowers decorated the middle of the table and sat on a yellow, handmade tablecloth. Karoline could tell that Kristina was a good housekeeper.

"Please, have a seat, and I'll heat up the coffee. I have some fresh kringle. Would you like one? And, if you don't mind, I'd like to check on my children. They are taking their morning nap."

With that, she set the coffeepot on the warm stove and whisked herself into the back room. Karoline took a peek at the rest of the house. It was just like the kitchen: clean, organized, and brightly decorated. When she returned, Kristina and Karoline sat down at the table. Karoline took a dessert and found it to be as excellent as her own.

"Did you just come from Norway? How long have you been in America?" Karoline asked.

"No, we moved here about ten years ago. We've been living on the East Coast. My husband has been working as a logger, and he heard there was cheap, fertile farmland in Iowa. What about you?"

"We've been living just north of you for about six years. We spent two years in Minnesota. My husband was a logger, too, and came to Iowa for the same reason. Tell me about your children."

"I have a boy and a girl, Halstein and Ingrid. He's three, and she's just under two. And you?"

"My daughter's name is Ingrid, too! I have six children, and as you can see, I'm due with another one sometime in January. I'll tell you them in order: Ingrid, Tingvald, Betsi, Alex, Gunda, and Sophie. The last two are twins."

"Tingvald? That's like the ship we came on."

Karoline couldn't resist relating the story of her first son's name. As she told the tragedy of Inger's death and Tingvald's birth on the ship, Kristina listened intently and inserted sympathetic comments. Karoline knew she was telling far more than one should on a first meeting, but she felt as though she had known Kristina for a long time. The petite woman's demeanor and smile felt warm and comforting. As much as she thought she should chatter only about the weather, she felt so drawn to her kindness and sympathy.

"Karoline, I don't know how you made it through all of that. You are the bravest woman. And you've got to be a saint to get through your trials. You remind me of my mother."

"I'm not sure how saintly I am. I'm out walking today so that I don't get too tempted to smother my husband. He's been laid up in bed for a month."

"Oh, my. You don't really think you'd smother him, do you?"

Karoline chuckled. "No," she said. "It's just been difficult lately." She then told Kristina about the recent horse escapade and her attempts to farm by herself. She even went as far as telling her about her son's berating.

At that point, Karoline decided she had been too personal and switched topics, asking about Kristina's family in Norway. They exchanged family heritages and news from home until they could hear children's cries coming from the bedroom.

"I need to get the children up. I've really enjoyed our time together. Do you think you could come again? Maybe tomorrow about this time? The children always take their morning nap around now."

"I would love to continue to visit. I'm not sure about tomorrow, but I'll try. Take care."

Karoline hurried through her chores the next morning. Once she made sure that Kristoffer had everything he needed, she took off and headed south. Kristina's door was open, and she was inside baking cookies.

"Good morning, Kristina. Are those oatmeal cookies I smell?"

"Good morning, Karoline. Yes, I made them hoping you would stop by. You have perfect timing. I just put the children down for their nap."

The two women settled themselves with coffee and cookies and began the conversation by talking about their children. Kristina told Karoline that she had endured a difficult birth with her last child and had almost died. The couple, with the midwife's advice, had decided to have no more children. Karoline said she thought this would also be her last one, and she was hoping for a boy.

The conversation again flowed easily. Each woman was sympathetic to the other as they shared trials and tribulations. As immigrants, nothing had been easy, and it seemed that every gain had cost them something valuable.

Karoline felt comfortable sharing more personal information as time slipped away. She said, "I wanted to ask about your husband. Mine seemed so loving when we courted but then turned stern and cold as we sailed farther away from Norway. Do you find the same thing with your husband?"

"Sometimes, yes," she replied. "When he decided to move here, he didn't consult me or ask me if I wanted to move. He just announced we were moving. Other times, he cares more about how I feel and wants me to agree with his decision."

"Kristoffer grew up in a strange family. Kristoffer, his father, bossed his wife. He also bossed the children. My father never acted that way."

"My father did. He saw it as his duty. He didn't think my mother was able to take care of herself or make decisions because he thought women were more like children. I think he believed that providing for them was a way to show love. He was not an affectionate man himself. I remember as a child, I would hug him, and I could feel him freeze up. He never actually hugged me; he just tolerated the hug I gave. We children were supposed to obey him without question, and he treated my mother the same."

"That sounds a lot like Kristoffer. He was very affectionate with the children when they were young, but as they've grown older, I've noticed the same kind of behavior you're describing. With me, he doesn't show much affection. I've been pregnant almost every year we've been married, but that isn't the same thing."

The women moved on to another topic at that point, but Karoline thought about this first part of their conversation for many days. She would have liked to talk to Kristoffer about what she had learned, but he was not the type of man who appreciated having conversations about feelings, especially his own. Her feelings toward him were different after that conversation. She tried to see from his perspective. Maybe he did love her and tried to prove that to her every day he walked out into the fields and toiled for his family.

Karoline tried to see Kristina once a week; however, there was so much to do in a day and not enough time. Often, weeks would pass without her having visited. Occasionally, Kristina brought her two children to Karoline's house so they could play with Betsi, Alex, and the twins.

Their conversations always started with something less personal but then evolved into their questions about men and marriage as well as their own pains and scars as wives and mothers. Karoline treasured each visit and found that it eased her heart to be able to pour out her concerns with an empathetic confidante. She had, once again, found a new Runa.

1892

Karoline gave birth to another son, and they named him after Kristoffer's grandfather, Ole. He was a large baby, weighing ten and a half pounds at birth. She labored for hours, which was actually a gift considering that it took Kristoffer longer to travel through the deep snow to fetch the midwife.

While Kristoffer sat on the edge of their bed, holding his newborn son, Karoline told him she wanted this one to be their last child.

"No," he replied. "We only have three sons with this one. What if something happens to one of them? I need sons to help me farm and then one day to take it over. This isn't like Norway. There is plenty of farmland to split among them. With more sons, I can buy more land."

She was too exhausted to argue with him at that point and let the topic drop. Though, she thought to herself, it takes two to make a child. He doesn't have complete say in this matter.

This birth had taken more out of her than the others. At twenty-seven, she did not recover quickly like she had the first time she'd given birth. She found herself too tired to keep going once she had prepared supper. Ole was a greedy baby, wailing to be fed what seemed like every half hour. Ingrid at eight and Betsi at four had taken over many of the house chores. Ingrid was even doing some of the laundry. Thankfully, the other children had outgrown the need for clouts, and there weren't as many of those to soak, scrub, and dry.

Spring planting came very early that year. March brought warm weather and solid rains. By early April, Kristoffer decided to plow the fields and plant, a full month earlier than usual. The price of corn had been high the last few years, so he chose to turn his wheat and oat fields to corn. They were no longer using the crops to feed themselves or their animals. It was far more lucrative to sell them in town. Kristoffer now farmed fifty acres, ten of which he'd bought last year on loan from the bank. With such a large farm, he hired extra hands in the spring and fall to help him.

Although he didn't actually need the little boy, Kristoffer declared that Tingvald was old enough to help him and woke his son at five-thirty each morning. Karoline couldn't argue that he was at the age when boys began working on the farm, but he also wasn't as large as other children. Instead of looking like he was a healthy seven-year-old, he looked more like a fragile five-year-old. She knew that it would do her no good to ask that he stay home: Kristoffer saw the boys as his responsibility to raise as proper men in his domain.

So Karoline took her girls to her domain, the garden. Even at three years old, the twins could contribute to their food production. As the family had grown, so had her garden mimicked that change. She planted lettuce and radishes nearest the house because they matured first. She put in four rows of peas, four rows of beans, twelve plants of tomatoes, six hills of squash, four hills of watermelon and four of muskmelon, seven rows of potatoes, and twelve rows of sweet corn. She even added pumpkins this year for both pies and carving. She placed all of the melons on the far end of the garden so their long vines would not reach out to her tomato plants or beans and ruin them. Her cornrows served as the mediator between her vines and her more fragile vegetables.

The planting done, Kristoffer and Karoline waited for the rains. Iowa generally had good rainfall through June. Once July came, there were fewer showers, and she relied on her rain barrels for watering the garden. Kristoffer had dug a well a year after they'd taken residence. Hauling water from a creek a mile and a half away gave him the impetus to put that on his list of very necessary things to complete. The well water supplied their household and laundry needs.

Kristoffer relied on his alfalfa fields to feed his animals through the winter and had put in enough this year to feed the extra cattle he had also bought with the loan money. His tender green shoots of corn poked through the soil very early and grew well with the spring moisture. The plants were already up to Kristoffer's calves and looked like they would be the best crop he had ever grown.

The last rain came on May 17. She couldn't call it a torrent or a shower; it was more like a drizzle. Every day after, the sun came out, and the sky was clear and blue. The heat clamped down on them earlier than usual. By early June, she woke up to eighty-degree weather, which peaked in the nineties by midday. The sun began to suck the moisture from the ground and turn the dirt dry. Day after day, the sun pummeled them until Karoline felt like her skin was going to crack from the lack of humidity.

By mid-June, every living thing needed rain. The corn stopped growing and the leaves were starting to darken and would eventually curl up in an effort to conserve water and retreat from the punishing sun. Karoline's garden looked the same. The family early on enjoyed several cuttings of lettuce and pulled up small flavorful radishes. The rest of the vegetable plants, which would mature in midsummer, started to sicken. The tomato plants were drooping, and her corn looked like their counterparts in the field. She and the children drew water from the rain barrels until they were empty. They then went back to drawing water from the creek. Kristoffer would not let them draw water from the well in the event that it too dried up. Eventually, even the creek went dry, and she had to watch as many of her plants turned yellow and eventually shriveled to nothing.

Every night, Kristoffer climbed out of their bed, and Karoline could hear him pacing the floor. Each morning, he left without eating breakfast and walked the fields, looking at the amount of damage the corn had sustained the day before. He didn't discuss his worries with her, but she could see the lines of concern forming on his face. He was worried about paying the loan on the new ten acres and cows. He was worried about providing for his family. And he could not make it rain. He could not make things better. He could only pace in frustration. She wanted to reach out to him and soothe his worries. She wanted to take some of the burden on herself, but she knew he did not think it was her place. As the provider of the family, he felt it was for him alone to solve.

On the Fourth of July, the family did not celebrate their new country's birthday. The corn had burned up to the point that it would take more effort to harvest it than it was now worth. Karoline fretted about how they would survive.

"Karoline, I'm going up north to find work," Kristoffer announced on the evening of the Fourth. "I'm going back to St. Paul to work in the mills. If I can find farm work before I reach St. Paul, I'll do that instead."

Karoline, stunned, said nothing. She was torn between having to run the farm by herself and knowing that his plan was probably the only way to survive until they could plant and harvest again. This was a time in which she needed to draw her own inner strength and pull her own share of the load.

"We can manage," she said. "There isn't much to do other than keep the animals alive. Tingvald can help me outside. Write to me when you arrive someplace so that I'll know where you are."

Three days after Kristoffer's departure, one of the Svensen brothers brought her a letter from town. Karoline was puzzled. The letter was from her mother and was posted May 2. Her father had suffered a heart attack. They found him in the field, dead. He had not returned at the end of the day, so the family had gone looking for him. The funeral services for him had taken place two months ago.

Karoline wept violently until she felt like her insides had been pushed out. Even though she hadn't seen him for several years, without him, she felt orphaned. Losing her parent was very different from losing her child. When she lost Inger, she'd lost a piece of herself. Losing her father felt like she was losing her compass. Even though he was a thousand miles away, she could still hear his voice telling her what she should do. Even the knowledge that he was out there had given her a sense of peace. In the letter, her mother told her there was a package coming for Tingvald.

Over the next few days, Karoline continued to think about her father. She was fixated on how her life had continued after he had already died. She thought about her conversations with Kristina, and while she was sitting there enjoying herself, her father was already cold in the ground. She thought about what she might have been doing the day he had passed. She couldn't remember exactly, but it was likely she'd been in the garden. It struck her how she had been trying to sustain life while her father was losing his. Her reflections carried her to the future, the day her husband would die. How would her children feel? Would they weep for him as she had for her own father? Would they feel that same sense of loss? Or would they feel cold and remember his harshness toward them? She imagined their brief weeping until they buried him and then their sense of relief that he was gone.

Karoline and Tingvald took care of the animals as well as they could. They drew just enough water from the well to sustain the beasts. Their milk cows were drying up. Their beef cows began dropping weight as they searched among the plant life, looking for grass among the growing weeds. Their horses' ribs were starting to show. Karoline felt guilty every time she went out to feed them. She could only give them enough food to keep them from dying. Their hay supply needed to be doled out sparsely.

She and the children suffered the same consequences. Without a garden, they didn't have much to supplement their meals. Usually, summer was a time of plenty. They enjoyed sliced tomatoes, fresh peas, and green beans. This year, she had promised the children muskmelon and watermelon. Kristoffer loved sweet corn and sat at the table with butter dripping down his face as he gnawed off row after row. In the fall, they ate squash. Karoline canned and pickled nearly the same amount for the coming winter.

How would they survive now? She had some potatoes and apples in her root cellar. There were still some canned tomatoes and string beans. However, none of it would last until next summer. Would they have to move? Instantly, the dugout invaded her mind. The dark, cold, damp hole in the side of the hill brought back anger and resentment. If they did move, she would never live that way again. They would be living in a wooden house or she and her children would be moving back to Norway. Having done it once, Norway now became her weapon.

Karoline packed away these worries and attended to real matters. She and the children needed to move the beef cows from one pasture to another. They had eaten down all of the grass and needed fresh pasture. These cows, unlike the milk cows, were wild and skittish of humans. She needed many bodies to push them in the right direction and get them across the way into the next pasture. Ingrid, Tingvald, Betsi, and Alex could help her while the three-year-old twins, Gunda and Sofie, could stand safely along the outside of the fence line, keeping busy with their dollies. She would put Ole in his sling, wrapped against her body.

With a solid plan in mind, Karoline took the children to the opposite side of the pasture so they could walk, arms out, toward the cows. She spread the five of them across the width of the land and started to walk, saying, "Hey cows, hey cows." She had warned the children not to be too loud or make any sudden moves. If they did, the cows would startle and run wildly, breaking the herd. When they had the cows close enough to the gate, she would send Alex to open it while she and the other children pushed them through. Her only apprehension was the distance between the two pastures. Would they continue straight into the next open gate? Or would they spook and take off?

As Karoline and her four children started herding the cattle across the pasture, her plan was working. The children followed her directions perfectly, and the cows trotted in the right direction. They stayed together and cooperated. As they neared the pasture's gate, Karoline signaled Alex to open it and stand behind it. The gate to the new pasture was open and ready to receive the animals. Once the leaders of the herd stepped up to the old gate, her plan fell apart. Her worries that they would take off in another direction came true. The first few cows stopped once they came to the gate entrance. The smaller hole scared them. To get them going again, Karoline waved her arms and started yelling at them. Because the back of the herd, pushed by Karoline, had nowhere to go but forward, the front of the herd was being forced to move as well. The cattle bunched up and started to panic. The leaders then jumped forward and took off to the right with the rest of the herd following. Alex jumped out from behind the gate and put his tiny four-year-old body in their path. Karoline screamed, "Alex, just let them go!" With all of the mooing and jostling of bodies, Alex didn't hear his mother. He stood his ground, arms out waving, and yelling at the cows to "get back."

Karoline could no longer see her small son and began to run. The cows no longer mattered. She could get more help and round them up later. As she came closer to the gate, she still couldn't see him. Once the cows cleared, she saw his trampled body lying in the dirt.

"Alex? Alex, can you hear me?" Karoline put her ear to his chest to listen for his heartbeat: it was faint. "Tingvald, saddle Millie and get the doctor. Ingrid, hook Charlie to the wagon and bring it here. Betsi, get the twins and Ole, go to the house, and put water on to boil. Cover the table with a clean sheet. Get out the bandages that your father used."

Each child jumped to the given task. Karoline sat down next to Alex, picked up his head, and laid it in her lap. She caressed his dark, curly hair and felt guilty. She prayed to God that He would not take another of her children. Old feelings came back to her. She had been in this situation before. A child of hers was dying, and it was up to her to make the decisions. Kristoffer was gone, probably near the same place he'd been the day Inger died. How had she come to this again?

Ingrid arrived with the wagon, and she and Karoline—putting their hands and arms under his body—tried to keep him as stable as they could while moving him to the wagon bed. Karoline stayed in the back with him while Ingrid drove as carefully as she could.

Arriving at the house, they used the same technique to bring Alex into the house and laid him on the table. Karoline listened for his heart again. He was still alive. She took cloths and wiped the grime from his face and body. With no medical experience, she could only sit and wait for the doctor.

The doctor, also an Olsen but no relation to them, arrived a few hours later.

"Karoline, Alex has some serious injuries," he informed her. "He has a few cracked ribs. I suspect he is probably concussed. His right arm is broken. His ankle is the worst. The bones are crushed. His ribs will heal on their own, and I can set the arm. But, I can't set his ankle. There is no other choice than to take his foot and ankle off."

Karoline gasped, put her hands over her mouth, and began to cry. This was her fault. She should have never had such a young child in a dangerous position. She pictured him with no foot, hobbling around on crutches. What kind of life had she just given him? What would Kristoffer say? He had already planned to give Alex part of the farm. Alex wouldn't be able to farm with a crutch.

"I don't have the supplies I need to remove his foot. I'll set the arm now so that it doesn't swell any more and wrap the ribs. I'll have to come back tomorrow for the foot. I'll leave you with some morphine to help with the pain."

The doctor wrapped the ribs firmly with bandages. He then aligned the bones in Alex's arm as best he could, wrapped a bandage around the break, and then put splints on it. He then wrapped the splints with bandages to keep them in place.

Karoline spent a long evening watching over Alex. She remembered his baby years and how he had cried so few times. He seemed to understand that she had plenty of worries, and he didn't want to be another one. He loved playing games of hide-and-seek with his siblings, and he often caught fireflies and brought them to her. His heart was so tender and good. That's why he'd stood in the middle of the cows' path. He was aware of how important it had been to get them to new grass. He just wanted to make her life easier. She cried again with guilt. With so many children, she hadn't had the time to give as much attention to the younger ones. Since Alex had always fussed the least, he had received the least amount of attention.

Dr. Olsen came again the next morning. The amputation required a great deal of medical skill. Dr. Olsen had served in the 21st Iowa Infantry Regiment during the Civil War as a surgeon and had experience with amputations. He gave Alex a quarter grain of morphine and made a weak solution of cocaine to inject into the main nerves of the leg. He asked Karoline to hold a rag doused with chloroform over Alex's nose and apply intermittently as he directed. Once ready, he cut the skin around the leg and then he took out his bone saw and started the hard work of amputating Alex's foot right above the ankle. Karoline could close her eyes to keep from seeing the grisly procedure, but she could not stop up her ears. She would be able to hear the sound of saw on bone for the rest of her life. She wished she was the one losing her foot instead of her child.

Once finished, they gently moved Alex back to his bed. The doctor left her with more morphine to get him through the next week or so. He promised to check on Alex every other day and told Karoline to send for him if she saw any negative changes in the boy.

Word of Alex's accident spread through Soldier. The Svensen brothers stopped at the house to see if there was anything they could do. Karoline asked them if they could take care of the missing cows. Some of them had come back and were in both of the pastures. Others were still wandering the countryside. They jumped to the task, rounding up other farmers to help out. When Kristina stopped by for a visit and found out about the accident, she went back home and put together a food basket for the family. The ladies at the Lutheran church, the one the family had attended sporadically, brought meat pies, pickles, assorted cakes, canned meat, and fresh vegetables. The community's generosity would feed them for a while.

Alex, drugged with morphine, slept through most days and nights. Karoline was thankful he wasn't in pain and didn't seem to understand the severity of his injuries. After three weeks, Dr. Olsen prescribed slowly taking away the pain medication. Karoline prepared herself for having to give Alex the news of his missing foot.

A letter from Kristoffer had also arrived and was brought to the house by a visiting church member. In the letter, he relayed that there had been no farm work, so he'd gone back to St. Paul. They were happy to see him and put him to work immediately. Kristoffer would be sending money when he could. When she received it, she was instructed to buy groceries in town along with hay for the animals. He had also sent a letter requesting a water diviner to find a place to dig a new well. He would be coming to the farm any day. He additionally dispatched a letter to the Svensen brothers to either dig the well themselves or hire someone to dig it. Karoline could tell that he was doing his best to take care of his family from afar.

Along with the letter, the church member also brought a wooden box from Norway. It was the gift her mother had sent Tingvald. Using a crowbar to pry open the crate, she saw inside, nestled among the packing materials, her father's black violin case. When Tingvald opened the case, the scent of her father drifted out. She laid her hand along the smooth red spruce body. Turning it over, she then ran her hand along the soft maple wood with the black striations. Karoline put her left hand on the fingerboard and her chin where her father's had been. She picked up the bow and ran it lightly across the strings.

"Mama, can I try it?" Tingvald begged.

"Of course. It's yours. Your *farfar* has given it to you. He was a very good violin player, and he has passed this along so that you too can play. Would you like that?"

He nodded quickly. She showed Tingvald how to rest his chin

on the wood, place his fingers on the strings, and hold the bow. She had never learned to play because her father thought that certain instruments were for women and others were for men. The violin was definitely played by a man.

Interested, Ingrid asked, "Can I try?"

"Yes, you may," Karoline replied, not believing in her father's division of musical instruments. "We need to find a teacher to teach you both how to play, but you need to remember that this belongs to Tingvald. Some day, Ingrid, you will also receive a gift from Norway. For the violin, you must always ask Tingvald for permission to play it. I'm just not sure where we're going to find you a teacher. I suppose I can reach out to some of our church friends and see if there is someone we can hire."

The violin kept the children occupied while Karoline waited for Alex to mend enough to know that he would not relapse or die. She would need to write to Kristoffer about the accident. She thought over the letter's contents and took her time composing it.

2 August 1892

Dear Kristoffer,

We were very pleased to hear from you and to know that you are doing well. Things here are as good as can be expected. We still have not received any rain. The crops continue to get worse. My garden is also losing many plants. I am anxious for the diviner to come and search for a new well site. I can then water my garden again.

The animals are doing well. We don't have much milk from the cows, but the rest of the animals are holding up. We moved the beef cows from the west pasture to the east one.

Sadly, my father passed away. My mother wrote of the death and funeral, which happened several months ago. I was distraught for several days but am starting to get used to his being gone. He sent Tingvald his violin. All of the children have enjoyed trying to play it. When times are better, I will search for a violin player who can give them lessons. It would be nice to hear music in the house once again.

My dear husband, I have sad news to tell you. Our Alex was trampled by the cows and has serious injuries. He has some cracked ribs and a broken arm. They will heal in time. The worst damage was done to his ankle. The bones were crushed, and the doctor had to amputate his foot above the ankle. He is in no pain and is healing well.

The accident happened when we were moving the cattle from one pasture to another. Alex was in charge of the gate and was safely behind it. Once the cattle turned and started running in the wrong direction, he put himself in their path in an attempt to stop them. I had no choice but to have our older children help with the cows. As you know, they are wild and take many bodies to control them. I am filled with sorrow and guilt over this unfortunate accident.

You do not need to come home or worry about us. We are all doing well. The doctor says Alex will be out of bed within a few weeks.

We think of you often. Be well. Hugs and kisses from the children.

Your Loving Wife,

Karoline

With trepidation, she waited for a reply. It did not take long to arrive. Kristoffer was furious with her. He berated her for having Alex in the cows' pasture. Didn't she realize what kind of danger she put the children in? Most of his letter informed her of the ruined future plans for their son. He also reminded her of his loss of a son to help him work the farm. He ended the letter by telling her that he would not be writing to her again. He would send money through the Svensens, and they would give her what she needed. They would also take care of purchasing the hay for the animals. Clearly, he was telling her that he no longer trusted her. He had turned over all financial responsibilities to the men. He finished his letter by telling her that he would see her when he returned in December. For once, Karoline was glad that he was not with her.

1905

Karoline arrived in Jefferson sometime in the middle of the afternoon. Iowa's heat had not relented, continuing to beat down on her and the horses. The vultures continued to follow her. Fortunately for her, but unfortunately for the farmers, rain had not fallen for her entire trip. Although the tarp was securely tied, it was not leakproof.

The dry heat reminded her of the summer that Alex had lost his foot. Kristoffer never contacted her again until his return. Karoline had been able to save some of the garden, losing all of her melons, though. The field corn lost its fight and burned to crisp, yellow stalks. Kristoffer wired money, the service a recent luxury in Iowa, to the Svensen brothers. She used store credit. The brothers brought hay to the farm for the animals. The drought of 1892 would have forced them to move if not for Kristoffer's working in the lumber mill again.

A few days before his return, he'd sent word of his impending arrival, and Karoline's stomach churned each day until he was due.

Her shoulders hunched in anticipation of a verbal assault. The children felt her nerves and crept about the house, keeping themselves small and unintrusive. Uncharacteristically, no squabbles erupted. A pall hung over them as though they were waiting for a funeral.

When Karoline heard the arrival of Kristoffer's horse, her stomach clenched into a tight fist. She could feel her legs shaking. She and the children stood at the door with smiles to welcome home their absent member. How would he treat her, she wondered?

Kristoffer walked through the door with a gust of wind. "Father's home," he announced. He kissed each child on the top of their head and walked past Karoline to put his things in the bedroom. The cold she felt was not from the winter weather.

That day, her marriage became very distant. Kristoffer only spoke to her of the children, intentionally avoiding any questions regarding her or them as a couple. When he left the house, his only words were "see you at supper" without kissing her or even looking at her. In bed, when she tried to lay her head on his shoulder, he quickly rolled onto his side, putting his back to her. For the first few months after his return, he primarily spoke to her through the children in the form of "tell you mother..." The winter, while always the longest period of the year, dragged on. Had the time been spring or summer, she might not have felt his rebuff so sharply; however, the winter trapped them inside, two warring animals in a cage.

Ingrid and Tingvald were old enough to understand why their father distanced himself from their mother. Karoline could tell that they were doing what they could to lighten the mood in the house. Both of them had picked up some skill on the violin. Although both clearly needed instruction, they could pluck out a few songs and sought to make their father laugh with their concerts. Betsi and the twins felt the tension in the house without understanding the reason for it. They cried and squabbled more frequently due the stress they held in their small bodies. Karoline ached the most for Alex. He knew he was the reason for the change in mood. Alex spent more time in his room, not wanting his father to see him on his crutches. And when he did see his father, Kristoffer never looked at Alex's missing foot, carefully looking the young boy only in the face.

The family suffered for four months. When the weather turned warm enough, they were all released from their frozen prison. Karoline and the girls turned to the garden; Kristoffer and Tingvald escaped to the fields. Putting their hands in soil medicated their suffering hearts. A renewed hope of new life through the fields and garden alleviated some of their hurt.

Alex, though, had no such opportunity. Karoline put him in a chair under a shade tree so that he could watch her and the others tilling and planting the new garden. Her guilt about his future gnawed at her even more. How would he make his way in this world? They were a farming people. Soldier was a farming community. They did not have the resources to send him to college to become a banker or a lawyer. They could not buy him a business like a mercantile or a seed store. Without a way to make a living, he would not marry or have a family. Karoline could picture him, living with them for the rest of his life. And she could not abide that picture. She could only make herself feel less guilty by finding him a future that fit him.

Kristoffer's anger and hostility faded a little with each passing month. Karoline and he were never as close again. They were now housemates instead of a married couple. They spoke of the children's needs. He thanked her for his meals. He never reached for her hand or touched her cheek. They continued to sleep in the same bed, but he seldom sought her body in the dark.

When Alex turned thirteen, Karoline began to search for an opportunity. As always, their friends assisted them. The Svensen brothers bought corn and wheat from the local farmers and sold it.

While a passenger train did not run through Soldier, they had managed to get a commodities train to stop. They now shipped their grain and sold it on the Chicago market. Farmers could also sell their beef cows the same way. Because Alex had shown an aptitude in math, Karoline had asked them if there was some job that Alex could do while sitting. He went to the grain elevator every Saturday during the school year and every day during the summer. Kristoffer seemed relieved not to see his son sitting in the shade while he and Tingvald went to the fields.

The brothers showed him how to fill out the commodities slips and keep track of sales. He picked it up quickly and became a permanent employee when he left high school. When Olof Svensen died, Elfred Svensen told Alex the opportunity to become his partner was his when he became old enough.

Kristoffer was proud of Alex's ability to excel at the skills needed to someday run the grain elevator successfully. Alex was becoming a respected member of the business community, and his opinion on corn futures was heeded by every farmer. Kristoffer was the first to seek out his opinions and followed them like they were the law.

Alex, now seventeen and engaged to Elizabeth, would be watching for Karoline's return with his father's body. Alex would have already arranged the funeral. Karoline felt a special bond with this son and leaned on him in times of need. She knew, though, that no matter how successful Alex became, her part in his changed life always stuck with Kristoffer like a thorn under his skin.

1895

On a cool but bright morning, Karoline was finishing feeding five-year-old Ole and had planned to start the morning dishes. Ole enjoyed his solo time with his mother when his siblings went off to school. They had nothing special planned for the day other than to wash some laundry and hang it on the line.

Karoline looked out the window and saw Olof Svensen driving his buggy up to the house. Karoline always enjoyed a visit from one of the Svensen brothers and put the coffee on the stove to reheat it while she searched the pantry for some kind of food offering.

"Karoline," Olof yelled from his buggy, "do you have time for some company?"

Karoline gladly invited him inside for a short visit. Whenever the Svensen brothers were near the farm, they always made a point of stopping to catch up. They never stayed longer than half an hour, which was just enough time to take a break and then resume her duties. Olof sat down at her kitchen table, put Ole on his lap, and kissed him on the cheek. Both of those men adored her children and often brought them treats and small gifts. Olof brought out of his pocket a small carved horse and handed it to Ole. Karoline was thankful that her children had adopted uncles with these two men. With her own brother and Kristoffer's family far away, sometimes it made her sad that her children did not have the army of immediate family that she and Kristoffer had enjoyed growing up.

Karoline noticed a rash around Olof's mouth and asked, "What's that rash around your mouth? How long have you had it?"

"I noticed it yesterday. It's probably from shaving off my winter beard and mustache. My tender skin hasn't seen the light since last October, and I often can get a rash from the razor."

To Karoline, it didn't look like a razor rash, but she said nothing more about it. Olof and Karoline caught up on Soldier news, and each of them enjoyed the other's company. He was especially animated in his tales of Chicago. He had just returned from a trip there to make contacts with their grain buyers. After that, his repertoire of conversational topics was limited to grain and cattle prices, his predictions for the new crops, and Alex's worthiness at the store. Karoline wasn't much interested in the first two, but she always enjoyed hearing how well Alex was doing. Almost to the exact minute of half an hour, Olof stood up and made his goodbyes. Karoline wished that he would stay a little longer because she enjoyed the company and wanted to put off the laundry just a little longer.

A few days later, Kristoffer came back from Soldier with news that Olof Svensen had fallen seriously ill. His mouth and neck were covered with fluid-filled blisters, and he had a high fever. Dr. Olsen diagnosed smallpox, and his brother Elfred moved to an empty stall in the barn so he wouldn't catch and spread the contagion. So far, no other community member had shown signs of the disease, which meant that Olof was the original spreader. The newspaper reported that Chicago was experiencing a smallpox outbreak, which was probably where he had contracted it.

Terrified, Karoline said, "Kristoffer, Olof was here three days ago. He sat at this table and had cookies with us. He kissed Ole on the head and gave him a toy that he had made. He may have infected us, too."

Kristoffer strode into Ole's room and woke the boy from his nap. He felt Ole's forehead and looked into his throat. "He doesn't have a fever, and his throat isn't red. I think he's fine. Do you feel well?

"Yes, I haven't noticed any changes in my health. I think we should go into Soldier and visit Dr. Olsen anyway. I would like to know more about this disease."

Dr. Olsen's waiting room was packed with frightened townspeople. Some had talked to Olof from across the street; others had been into the feed store and bought items from him. His usual patience waning, Dr. Olsen explained to the patients that they had no risk since many of them had not been near enough to him or had briefly exchanged a few words. None of them had been with him long enough or had taken personal items from him to warrant such panic.

When it came time for Karoline and Kristoffer's turn, his exasperated tone turned into authentic concern. The length of the visit and proximity made both her and Ole vulnerable. Ole, having received a kiss and a hand-made toy, was in the greatest danger.

Karoline worried about Kristoffer and the children. They had been in close quarters. Of course, she had kissed each child before they had gone to bed. Even Kristoffer still received a polite peck on the lips at bedtime. They could all die from this outbreak.

"Karoline, you don't need to worry about the other children. You are not contagious unless you get the rash. If you or Ole have the pox, you won't see anything for two weeks or more. Right now, neither one of you is contagious, but I think you should find somewhere else to live for a while. I'll come out to your house in two weeks to check on you. I don't want either of you to be with people, and I think just to be safe, the children should stay home from school until this passes," Dr. Olsen advised.

Kristoffer, as usual, took charge of the situation. He decided that he and the children should go elsewhere so that if Karoline and Ole did become infected, they would have the comfort of their own home.

While Karoline waited for the disease to come barging in their door, she continued to get reports of Olof. The pox had moved down to cover the entire trunk of his body as well as his legs. They covered the inside of his mouth and throat. The pustules engorged with fluid. His fever climbed, and his glands enlarged. Olof complained of a raging headache and body aches. Dr. Olsen administered morphine to abate the pain enough for him to sleep. Elfred, however, showed no signs of getting ill, which encouraged Karoline.

Kristoffer stopped by twice a day, once in the morning and once in the evening, to check on them. He filled her water buckets and took care of her garden. He brought her news from town, especially regarding Olof's progression of the disease. For once in their marriage, he was concerned, solicitous, and sympathetic to his wife and child.

Every morning, Karoline scrutinized Ole's body, looking for any rash. She felt his forehead against her own to determine if he had a fever. She prayed fervently to any god who might listen to spare her child and herself. Exactly fourteen days from Olof's visit, Ole spiked a high fever but had no rash. Karoline hoped that this was some other illness. Her son also complained of body and headaches. Maybe, Karoline hoped, it was the flu.

Two days later, Ole complained to her that the inside of his mouth was sore. When she looked inside, she saw small red spots on his tongue and down his throat. She, too, now felt a headache and body aches. While she wanted to continue to diagnose the flu, she was a practical enough woman to recognize that they both had contracted smallpox.

Karoline discovered her own rash two days after Ole's. Like his, hers started inside her mouth and spread down her throat. Like her son, she too suffered from terrible headaches, fever, and swollen glands. She put her own misery aside as best she could to minister to her son. His rash was now on the outside of his body, starting on his face and going down his torso. As she watched her son progress with this disease, she could foretell her own fate.

By the fourth day, his bumps were starting to fill with fluid and were spreading further over his body. His entire face, neck, torso, arms, and legs were covered. He cried through the day and night, and she could do nothing to alleviate his pain.

Kristoffer checked on them in the evening, and with a mouth full of blisters, she could not respond when he called for her. His face, covered with a cloth, appeared in their bedroom door where she and Ole were suffering. Unable to walk between her own room and Ole's, she thought it best to put them into the same bed. "Karoline, are you ill as well?" he asked. She could only nod her head.

Kristoffer left and returned again, his face with two coverings, bringing a bowl of cool water and a fresh cloth.

"Dr. Olsen told me that I need to keep this face covering on at all times and wash my hands often if I needed to take care of you. I will stay in the house. You don't need to do anything. I can take over now."

A rush of relief flowed through her body. She had gotten to the point that she could no longer stand for very long, her muscles no longer seeming to work. For the first time since she'd left Minnesota, she put herself completely back in Kristoffer's hands and allowed him to take care of her and make all the decisions.

Kristoffer started by cooking scrambled eggs, the only thing he knew how to prepare. Karoline didn't care what he made as long as she didn't have to do it. However, neither she nor Ole was hungry. With blisters in their mouths, eating was impossible.

As the days passed, Kristoffer hustled in and out of the bedroom. He made sure to keep fresh water by her bed. As she went in and out of sleep, she recognized at times that he was making her drink water. He was doing the same for Ole. Kristoffer kept wet compresses on their foreheads to help with the fever. Each time she was awakened by his activity, she could see worry in his eyes.

Both of their pustules continued to fill, but Ole's were far worse than hers. Many places on his body were one large blister as they grew into one another. Karoline felt her throat swelling as they expanded, which made breathing more uncomfortable; however, she did not have as many on her face as Ole did.

Thirteen days into their illness, Ole stopped crying, speaking, and drinking. His fever raged, and his body had become one big pustule. Kristoffer brought Dr. Olsen to the house, but he told them there was nothing he could do for the boy but wait it out. Kristoffer was told to wet fresh sheets and drape them over Ole's naked body. Keeping him as cool as possible became their only strategy.

Karoline felt her motherly need to protect her child tugging at her, but she could do no more than watch him from her side of the bed. Kristoffer changed sheets twice a day, washing the old ones in lye soap to kill the contagion. His exhaustion hung on him like an old pair of overalls. Karoline had never seen this side of her husband. This was the person she thought she had married.

On the fifteenth day, Karoline woke in the early morning. She could not hear her son breathing. Panicked, she screamed, and

Kristoffer flew into the room. Her face announced her concern, and he listened to Ole's chest. Kristoffer sat down on the bed, covered his eyes, and bent over. Karoline knew her son was dead. Kristoffer wrapped Ole in the sheet and said, "We will bury him in the Lutheran cemetery when you are well again. I will take care of everything."

Karoline's recovery started when the pox began to form a crust and scab over. She was so deep in her grief that she did not notice or care about her own progression. Losing Ole brought back the same pain she'd felt with Inger. Her heart hurt, and her body felt like an empty cornhusk. Her children had been farmed out to various neighbors and church friends, so she did not even have the comfort of continuing to mother them.

Kristoffer continued his ministrations to her, and he tried his best to comfort her. A heavy sweater of grief hung on him, almost drowning him and weighing him down. Karoline wondered why he had not been this way when their first child had died. Was it because he had lost a son instead of a daughter? Was it because he hadn't known Inger as well? In some ways, Karoline felt bitterness against him because he seemed more devastated by this loss, but she knew that it was wrong to feel this way. Kristoffer suffered for his son the same as she. The realization of her own feelings signaled to her that her anger against him, even eight years later, remained raw.

Twenty-two days from Ole's first symptoms, Karoline crawled out of her bed and stood on her feet. Her legs felt weak. She wanted to see her children.

"Kristoffer, I feel well enough to have the children home again. Dr. Olsen said I am no longer contagious. I just need to wrap my arms around them and put my nose into their hair. I... need something to help me want to go on living."

"They want to come home as well. I will round them up today while you give yourself a bath. I will boil water for you and fill up the tub. We're going to burn the bedding. Dr. Olsen said that since you haven't been anywhere in the house since you fell ill, the pox would not catch onto anyone else. We will need to scrub this room, though."

"I've been meaning to ask you about Olof Svensen. How is he? He's probably still weak like me?"

"I'm sorry, Karoline. I didn't want to tell you at the time. Olof died a week before Ole. I thought that it wouldn't have done you any good to know, and I was worried it would frighten you."

"I feel terrible. That poor man. He was so good to our children and us. Did anyone else in the town get it?"

"No. Dr. Olsen thought that the wooden toy that Olof gave Ole was probably the reason he became ill. We both thought that Ole probably put it on his face. I know how much he likes to rub soft things on his skin. And, of course, Ole passed it to you."

"Olof also kissed Ole on his head. You know how much those two bachelors love our children. Kristoffer, a kiss probably killed our son."

"I don't want to talk about this anymore. I have the funeral plans made, and the coffin is finished. Whenever you feel well enough, we can go ahead with it."

Over the next two days, Karoline regained enough strength to pull together funeral clothes. Ingrid, Betsi, Gunda, and Sofie made the house presentable for the visitation; however, since the house had been plagued with pox, Karoline and Kristoffer decided on a grave-side burial only. To Karoline, it seemed wrong to send her child off with only a few prayers, as she had done for Inger. She had never thought of Kristoffer and herself as unfit parents who could not give their loved ones proper burial rites. Karoline imagined her own father's visitation with their neighbors and church community sitting up with their mother in the parlor. Food would have decorated the kitchen. Hushed tones drifting through the house would have blended in with quiet crying. Her father's funeral marked the end of his life, and she was sure that it must have reflected the dignified way he carried himself through this world.

Ole's graveside burial occurred on a Wednesday afternoon in the rain. No community members, no church friends—only the immediate family and Elfred Svensen attended the service. Karoline had not expected more but had hoped there would be more mourners, but people were afraid that they would contract the contagion. Even though Dr. Olsen had stood up in church and had explained how it was contracted, superstition always won out over science. Ole's grave would stand alone in the Olsen section in the Soldier Lutheran Church's graveyard until the next family member would join him. Karoline wished so badly that they could bring Inger to Soldier to lie beside her younger brother. It pained her to have her daughter lying by herself so far away from her family.

1901

Ingrid, a month shy of her seventeenth birthday, asked her parents for permission to marry. She and Stefan Andersen had fallen in love at one of the annual church picnics. Stefan—blonde, blue-eyed, and twenty-two years old—worked as a farmhand for another Norwegian family. Karoline, concerned about Ingrid's age, now could put herself in her parents' place. She understood why they had insisted she wait until she was eighteen. Kristoffer, though, had never agreed with her parents' reasoning; he saw nothing wrong with a woman marrying at sixteen or seventeen. Kristoffer and Karoline gave their consent. They planned a June wedding before the Iowa heat arrived.

Karoline and Ingrid started to prepare immediately. As soon as the ground warmed enough to grow seeds, they planted the flowers for her bouquet. Ingrid wanted white and yellow daisies. Karoline took her wedding dress from her traveling trunk. Although yellowed with age, Ingrid still wanted to wear it. When she tried it on, the dress was a bit large through the shoulders and a little long. Karoline soaked the material in water and soap, which took out the yellowing, and began the process of refitting it. She was pleased that her daughter would wear her dress. As she worked on the garment, she was transported back to her own wedding day.

Karoline had disputed with her mother Armaliea over that wedding dress. Norwegian girls were gifted hand-made *bunads* when they were sixteen or seventeen. These national costumes were designed specifically for each region. Karoline's *bunad*, like her mother's, comprised a long, black skirt; crisp, white blouse; long, white apron with designs along the bottom; and a vest with a chest plate, embroidered with floral designs. Norwegian women wore their *bunads* for special occasions—and always at their weddings. Armaliea expected Karoline to wear her *bunad* as did every other young woman. Karoline, though, desired to follow the new trend, which was started by Queen Victoria, and wear a white dress and veil. Having only two daughters, Armaliea relented to her daughter's wish.

Armaliea designed the dress with short, puffy sleeves, a squared neckline, an empire waist, and a short, rounded train on the back. Several rows of lace panels adorned the front and followed the hemline all the way around. The body of the dress was made from white linen, and she attached a gauze overlay, making the sleeves from the same material. The sheer veil attached to the back of Karoline's head and went down several inches past her fingertips.

Her mother worked for weeks, hand-sewing the dress. After its completion, she added undergarments to her daughter's trousseau. While Armaliea worked on these items, Karoline finished sewing her house linens: a tablecloth, dishtowels, and blankets. She had been preparing her wedding necessities since she was nine, storing all of her keepsakes in a cedar chest. Since everything was required to fit into her traveling trunk, she was limited in what she could bring with her.

On the morning of May 27, Karoline arose to a beautiful but cool day. Breakfast smells pulled her out of bed. Her mother brewed fresh coffee and laid out bread with butter and homemade berry jam. Since it was a special occasion, Armaliea also made fried eggs. She thought the family needed more sustenance since the day would be long.

After getting Karoline into her wedding attire, her mother wrapped a blanket around her and put her on the seat next to her father. The rest of the family climbed into the back of the wagon.

Arriving at St. Olaf Lutheran Church, Karoline felt her stomach flutter in excitement. Although the service would be very small, mostly the two families, her nerves mixed with her excitement. She had asked Runa to stand up for her, and Kristoffer had asked his brother Volter.

Standing in the back of the church with her father and Runa, Karoline waited for the rest of the guests to arrive. Kristoffer stood with Volter in front of the church. He looked handsome. He wore a black suit he'd borrowed from his uncle, his dark, wavy hair had been brushed and oiled, and his dark beard and mustache were neatly trimmed. She couldn't believe that such a striking man would be her husband.

Her father surprised her by asking, "Are you sure you're ready to be married? You can postpone this."

"Yes, I'm very sure. I love Kristoffer, and he loves me. We have our future planned. We know what we're doing."

Saying her vows and promising to love, honor, and obey came from her lips as sweetly as music. She and Kristoffer were to become one, their love and commitment bound by the law of both man and God. She felt so proud and sure in that moment. She imagined their lives stretched out before them: a fertile farm with black soil and growing crops, children running about the house, and the two of them deeply in love and growing old together. Karoline looked purposefully into Kristoffer's eyes and said, "I do," with with as much conviction as she had ever felt about anything.

With vows given, Kristoffer kissed her in front of their families and whispered, "I love you," into her ear. Their reception consisted of desserts and coffee in the church basement. Kristoffer stayed by her side, never allowing his hand to stray from her hand or waist or elbow. Every time she looked at him, he was already looking at her. He often whispered compliments and endearments of love into her ear while she was waiting to speak to the next guest. She saw Kristoffer's father scowl and shake his head at his son. She assumed he was displeased by the public display of affection, especially in a house of worship.

They spent their wedding night at her Aunt Anja and Uncle Daniel's house because it was closer to the church and had spare rooms. They would have more privacy than they would in her bedroom at home.

Finally with some time alone, Karoline and Kristoffer began their life as a married couple. Kristoffer offered to take off her boots and unbuttoned each one of them. He held up her foot and said, "Did I just marry a gal with big feet?"

Karoline giggled and replied, "*Ja*. And wait until we have girls with big feet, too. We'll never get any men to marry them."

He kissed the bottom of her right foot and told her to stand while he helped her remove her wedding regalia. Her dress was decorated with a long row of pearl buttons running down the back. Her mother had buttoned them, and now her husband must unbutton them. His large, calloused fingers gently ran each button through its hole. Once her dress was removed, Kristoffer marveled at the underclothes a woman wore: a corset and pantaloons covered by a chemise and long petticoat with long stockings held up by garter belts. He took his time and unwrapped his present, layer by layer. Once naked, Karoline—too shy to stand in front of him—darted for the bed and slid under the blankets. Kristoffer stood in front of her and removed his shirt and pants. As soon as he started to remove his drawers, she put the covers over her head. From under the covers, she could hear him chuckling at her embarrassment. Lamps turned down, Kristoffer crept under with her. He laughed as he wrapped his cold body around hers to warm himself as she squealed and tried to get away. He held her close and stroked her hair and cheek.

"I don't ever want to hurt you," he said. "You are more than my wife: you are my life. We will go to America and build our dream together. I can't even tell you how much I love you. We will be together for the rest of our lives."

She felt completely connected to him and allowed him to take her body and connect them physically.

As Karoline sat shortening the hem on her wedding dress, she wondered again how they had gone so wrong. One of her motherly duties was to prepare her daughters for their marriages, including the wedding night. What should she say to Ingrid? You never know a man until the honeymoon is over? Don't get too attached to Stefan because he'll probably break your heart? Karoline should not be so cynical about marriage to this young girl in love. She would only ruin the relationship between her daughter and herself if she was truthful. It would be better to give her advice on how to keep a marriage going and hope that it was better for her.

Ingrid looked beautiful the day of her wedding. Her dark, curly hair had been intricately braided so that the individual braids were looped together to make a cascade down her back. Karoline inserted white daisies across the band of her veil. The dress, simple yet elegant, suited Ingrid well. Stefan, wearing a dark suit, was clean-shaven and wide-eyed. Like her own ceremony, Ingrid promised to love, honor, and obey her husband. Karoline could not help but think about the word *obey*. She had not thought about it much when she'd said it, but now she was hearing her daughter promise to obey, and it struck her as wrong. Within the vows themselves, women were set up as an animal or a child. Men did not have to promise the same thing. From day one, women were relegated to a station beneath men. She put away those thoughts as the ceremony ended because she did not think it was appropriate to dwell on such negative feelings. This was to be a happy day.

Their guests were served a variety of cakes and coffee in the church basement. She saw Kristoffer take Stefan outside, and they did not return for almost an hour. She wondered what he could be telling this young man. Wasn't it Stefan's father's place to speak to him about the wedding night?

Instead of returning to Stefan's house for the wedding night, Ingrid and Stefan decided to go on a honeymoon trip, something couples were beginning to do. They would be going to Sioux City for two days. Stefan had family living there, so they could stay with them. Stefan borrowed a buggy from a friend so that he and Ingrid would not need to take a farm wagon. Once they changed out of their wedding clothes, their families saw them off.

Karoline waved to them until they disappeared and then turned to Kristoffer.

"What did you say to Stefan? Were you giving him marriage advice?"

"That isn't my place. I'm sure his father took care of that. I was talking to him about living on our farm and farming with me. Since Alex will never farm, I thought that Stefan could take his place. I need the help, and he can quit working for someone else. He can earn his acres. The couple can live with us until they get their own house built. I'm sure you would like Ingrid to stay near us."

Karoline smiled and hugged Kristoffer. "I would love that."

It had been too long since Kristoffer had shown his affection, but he returned her smile and patted her back.

1904

Karoline, sitting across from Betsi, looked dumbfounded. She wasn't sure that she had heard her daughter correctly.

"What did you just say to me?" she asked.

"I'm with child," Betsi said while looking at her feet.

"How did this happen? And, I don't mean the physical part of it. Who is responsible for this?"

"Jimmy Sullivan." Betsi continued to stare at her shoes, not wanting to look into her mother's eyes.

Karoline sat quietly for several minutes. She was not trying to make her daughter nervous, but if she did, it was probably appropriate. So many questions popped into her head that she could not answer: Where? When? Was this her fault as a mother? She realized that the where and when probably didn't matter since the answers didn't change the circumstance. She moved from thinking about the act itself to thinking about Kristoffer's reaction. She thought that he would probably make the boy marry Betsi. It was what was done in this type of situation.

"You need to tell your father tonight when he comes home." She could see the frightened reaction on Betsi's face. Karoline herself was frightened for her daughter. There would inevitably be some type of explosion. He had never beaten one of his children, but that didn't mean that he wouldn't. They had never given him cause to do so. This, however, was completely different.

"Can't you tell him for me?" Betsi pleaded.

"I understand your fear, but if you are adult enough to get yourself into this condition, then you are adult enough to tell him."

Karoline went about the rest of her day. She scrubbed mounds of dirty clothes and turned around to scrub mounds of dirty dishes. She normally did not attend to the dishes—that was Betsi's job—but she wanted to complete simple tasks so that she could think about this newest problem. Betsi fortified herself in her room, and Karoline thought it best that she remain there. The other children did not need to see her red, puffy eyes. They would only want to know what problem had caused Betsi to cry so much.

One piece of laundry after another, one dish after another—Karoline continued to roll Betsi's pregnancy around in her brain. Betsi must have met this boy at school. Since he was Irish, Karoline assumed he was Catholic, so she certainly hadn't met him at a church function. The children didn't go out to social functions without their parents, so how had she spent so much time with him? Karoline's mind slipped to the sexual act, and she wondered where they had gone to get the privacy they would have needed. And, why hadn't she noticed Betsi's missing blocks of time? She supposed that because she still had six children to attend to, she could not know every movement they made. Karoline knew these details would be forthcoming: Kristoffer would want them. He always got what he wanted.

Kristoffer walked into the house promptly at 6:15, the same time as every evening when he wasn't in the fields. After he washed up, the family, minus Betsi, sat down to a supper of fried ham, fried potatoes, and baked apples.

"Where is Betsi?" he asked. "Is she sick?"

"Somewhat," Karoline replied. "We need to deal with something after supper. For now, just eat."

Kristoffer's face showed his dismay and lack of understanding, but he said no more and finished the supper in peace. While Karoline and the twins washed the dishes and tidied up the kitchen, Kristoffer and Alex discussed the day's events and markets. When Karoline finished her kitchen chores, they sent the rest of the children to their rooms.

Karoline, Kristoffer, and Betsi sat at the kitchen table. Betsi's white face contrasted starkly with her red, puffy eyes.

"What is wrong with you?" Kristoffer asked.

"I'm with child," Betsi said almost inaudibly.

Kristoffer looked over at Karoline, and she could tell that Kristoffer hadn't heard Betsi's reply.

"She said she's with child," Karoline repeated for him. The words dropped to the floor and disappeared into the cracks while Kristoffer sat still, staring at his daughter. Karoline could see the red starting to creep up his neck and into his face. A vein in his temple bulged out, and she could see it throb with each heartbeat. The longer he said nothing, the more afraid Karoline became. Even though they had been married for twenty-one years, she truly did not know what he would do. She feared that he would strike Betsi.

"Who did this to you?" he demanded loudly, slamming his hand on the table, making the cups and saucers jump.

"Jimmy Sullivan."

"He's Irish," he spat out. "Why were you with an Irish boy? How old is he?"

"Sixteen. He's a boy at my school."

"Girl, you had better start talking and tell me how this happened. Did he rape you? Did you fight him?"

"No! He's just a boy I like. Sometimes he walks me part way home from school. He didn't force himself on me."

"Walking you home isn't going to get a baby. Where did he take advantage of you?"

"In the tall grass along the path."

"There hasn't been tall grass since last fall." Kristoffer looked over at Karoline, and she knew what question he wanted answered but didn't want to ask.

"When was the last time you bled?" she asked.

"November, maybe December?"

"That means you are somewhere around four or five months along," Karoline said.

"I don't know." Betsi could take no more grilling from her father and laid her head on the table, her arms wrapped around her head, and she began to cry.

"You are a disgrace to this family! Go to your room and don't come out. I don't want to look at you anymore!"

Once Betsi had secured herself away, Kristoffer turned to Karoline. "How long have you known this?"

"She told me today."

"Do you know who this boy is? Do we know who his parents are?"

"No. You know how this community is. Each kind sticks together. How many people do we know who aren't even Norwegian?"

"He's Catholic!" Kristoffer realized. "She can't marry a Catholic! And everyone knows that Irish are drunkards. This is a disgrace. Our family will suffer for this. If he was Norwegian, we could say that they were madly in love and eloped. That's believable. But to marry an Irish? No. Everyone in our church, in our community, will know what happened. It's just not done. We will be those terrible parents who allowed their daughter to run loose. Our good name will be blackened. She can't marry him."

"Are you thinking we should send her away? Who would we send her to? Your brother and his family now live here. Sophie is in Chicago. Should we send her there?"

"If we send her away, everyone will know why. Remember two years ago when the Nilsens sent away their daughter? What is the first thing we all thought? If your daughter leaves your house, she is either marrying or working on another farm within the community. I need to think about this for a few days. Betsi doesn't leave this house. Do you understand? You also need to find out if she told that Irish boy."

Betsi had not told Jimmy Sullivan. "Am I going to marry him?" she asked Karoline, hope lighting up her blue eyes.

"No. People stick to their own kind. You are Lutheran, and he is Catholic. You are not going to disgrace us by becoming Catholic. I don't understand why you were with someone who wasn't part of our community. There are plenty of Norwegian boys from good families. How could you have done this to us? How could you have so little respect for yourself? I taught you better than this."

"What's going to happen to me? Am I going away?"

"I don't know. This is your father's decision as head of this house. You should probably stay away from him until he decides what to do. Every time he looks at you, he is disappointed."

Betsi took her mother's suggestion and kept herself in her room when her father came into the house. Karoline did not press Kristoffer for his decision. She waited for several days, knowing he would tell her first. Those days were filled with tension. It pervaded every corner of the house. The children seemed to feel that something was horribly wrong and had learned long ago to stay quiet and out of the way. Karoline hated to see her children creep around the house, afraid of their father. She had never felt such an atmosphere in her own home. She thought about what her own father would do in this situation. She couldn't imagine either herself or Sophie daring to have relations outside of marriage. Kristoffer hadn't even asked her for more than a kiss. What kind of family were these Sullivans? Did they not raise their sons to be gentlemen? This surely was another reason to deny marriage to this boy.

After three days, Kristoffer finally told her his plan while they were lying in bed. "We will do away with this mistake."

"Put it up for adoption?"

"No. We must eradicate it now, before it grows any bigger. I will go tomorrow and talk to the midwife. She's a good Norwegian. She will understand and help us. This is the only way to save our name, to save our daughter's reputation."

Kristoffer wouldn't say the word—*abortion*. Karoline did not understand what he meant for a second or two. When she finally understood his meaning, she sat up in bed. "No, you can't kill her child, our grandchild. It's wrong."

"I'm not going to argue with you. I have made my decision. I am head of this house, so we will do this." He turned his back to her and pretended to fall asleep.

Karoline lay awake through the night. She never imagined that he could go through with something so extreme. He expected her to maintain a united front in this, and she couldn't. She had spent most of her adult years protecting life. She had failed her first daughter, and she hadn't protected her son well enough. She couldn't stand the thought of failure again even though she didn't have a plan to solve the problem without losing their good name.

Kristoffer left in the morning to speak to the midwife but came home again within an hour. Karoline could tell that something had not gone well.

"What did she say?"

"She said that she only brings live babies into this world. She refuses to perform any other services that go against that conviction. She wouldn't even discuss it with me. She asked me to leave her house."

"Do we send Betsi away?" Karoline asked hopefully.

"I already said there was only one solution to this problem. If the midwife won't help us, then I will find someone who will. After lunch, I'm going into town to see Dr. Olsen. He's helped our family before."

Kristoffer left after lunch and didn't return until after supper. His face, resolute and calm, told her that he had found the solution.

"Did Dr. Olsen say that he would perform the procedure?"

"No, but he did sympathize with us. He gave me the name of a woman in Castana who does these things. I went to see her, which is why I'm home late. She is coming to see Betsi tomorrow. She has some questions about how far along she is." Before Karoline could ask him any questions about this woman, Kristoffer walked out the door and stayed in the barn until she had gone to bed.

In the late morning, a woman in a buggy pulled up to their house. Karoline knew who she was. She wanted to tell the woman that they didn't need her services or that she had the wrong house, but she didn't dare go against Kristoffer. Karoline stepped out the door to greet her before anyone saw her. They hadn't told Betsi that decisions had been made.

"Good morning. I am Karoline Olsen."

"Good morning, ma'am. I'm Hannah Schiltz. Your husband

asked me to visit."

Hannah Schiltz stood at least a foot taller than Karoline. She wore a black bonnet, shawl, and skirt. Her eyes were piercing blue, and she too had blonde hair, like Kristina. She carried a case in her hands, and Karoline didn't want to look at it. She did not want to imagine the kinds of things that might be in there to do the job that Hannah Schiltz had come for.

"I would like to examine your daughter. Your husband informed me of her trouble and how long she may have been in this trouble. If she's too far, I won't perform the procedure. May I come in?"

"Of course." Karoline showed her into the kitchen and asked if she would like a cup of coffee. "I need to get Betsi. She doesn't know anything about this. Please sit down."

Karoline sent the other children outside to complete chores. She brought Betsi into the kitchen.

"This is Mrs. Schiltz. She's here to examine you. We'll go into your bedroom."

"Examine me for what?" Betsi asked as her mother was ushering her toward her bedroom.

"Betsi," Hannah Schiltz said, "I want you to lie back on your bed, lift your shirt up and push your skirt down some. I want to look at your stomach."

Betsi complied while looking at her mother. Karoline could tell that she now understood that this examination had something to do with her pregnancy. Karoline also wondered if Betsi had noticed that she hadn't called the woman a doctor, not that anyone would have thought that a woman was a doctor.

Hannah Schiltz pressed her fingers into Betsi's stomach. She then put her ear on it and listened.

"Have you felt the quickening?"

Betsi looked at her mother for clarification. "Have you felt the baby move?" Karoline explained.

"I'm not sure. What would I feel?"

"If feels like a fluttering," Karoline said. "Have you felt anything that you don't usually feel?"

"I don't think so."

Karoline and Hannah Schiltz left Betsi lying in her bedroom and went to the kitchen. They both sat at the table with cups of coffee between them. Hannah's voice was soothing and kind. If not for their circumstances, Karoline thought that they could have been friends.

"Betsi is further in her pregnancy than your husband said. Another week, and it would be too late. A larger baby is more difficult to dispel. This is going to be very hard on the girl."

Karoline wanted to ask the woman to lie and say that it was already too late, that she wouldn't do the procedure because it was too dangerous. She didn't know this woman well enough to ask such a favor. Knowing how staunch Kristoffer's feelings were, Karoline felt like she had no choice but to go through with his plan.

"I need to speak to your husband about my fee. It will be more than I said. Is he around?"

"He's feeding cattle and won't be home for two to three hours."

"I have some errands I can complete in Soldier. I will be at the Soldier Café around four. Please ask him to meet me there."

Karoline waited for Kristoffer to come for lunch. While she waited, a new plan came to mind. She didn't know why it had not come to her before now. It would solve the problem and save the child.

When Kristoffer walked in for lunch, he looked at her with a questioning face. He wanted to know if the situation had been resolved.

"She said that it would be more money and wants to meet you at four in the Café, but I have another way. We don't have to do this.

We can say that the baby is ours. We'll keep Betsi inside until she delivers. That way no one will ever know that she carried a child. I can wear some extra petticoats to add more bulk. I can also stay around the house so that no one would know that I wasn't expecting another child."

Kristoffer looked at her, his face dumbstruck. Karoline couldn't tell whether he was pleased that she had thought of another way out or if he was upset that she was still trying to change his plans.

"Why won't you support me in this?" Raising his voice, he continued, "Why won't you just do as I say? I will never claim an Irish bastard for my own! No more! I will not discuss this or wait any longer. I don't care how much money it costs me. She will have this procedure tomorrow!" With this last statement, he brought his fist down onto the table again.

"I understand." Karoline went about bringing his lunch to the table. Instead of sitting with him, she left the house and went and looked at her empty garden. She had not started the spring planting yet, but the soil stood ready for the seeds. She could see into the future when her plants would be green and healthy. The cycle of fallow ground to fertile soil germinating the seeds transpired each year, reminding Karoline of her own womb.

But it was not her own womb that she now focused on. Betsi's seed would be ripped from her soil before it had a chance to become healthy and grow to its intended potential. Karoline thought about all of her children and what life would have been like without them. Each child mirrored the other but had their unique traits. Each child was a plant in her garden. Each played a role in the family, and their sum made her heart complete. She believed that each of her children would grow into their destiny. Outside of their own family, they had their own roles to play. What was Betsi's child's destiny that would go unfulfilled?

When Kristoffer returned for supper, he said, "It's done. She's coming back tomorrow to complete the procedure. You need to have Betsi ready. She will come again late morning, and I will stay home with you."

Lying in bed next to Kristoffer, Karoline couldn't sleep, thinking about what tomorrow would bring. She turned from her back to her side to her back again, trying to find a comfortable position.

"I know you're upset about Betsi, and you don't agree with me," Kristoffer said from out of the dark. "I love our daughter, too. I'm angry with her for putting all of us in this impossible position. I wish things were different. I've tried thinking of every way that we can get out of this without losing something. Every time I would look into its eyes, I would see the mistake that Betsi made. I would think of that child as her disgrace. I couldn't love it. I'm afraid that I would stop loving her."

Karoline did not respond. She turned back to her side and let her tears slide quietly down her face. How could a father stop loving his own child? Who was this man who could turn off his love for his own blood? She too had disappointed him, and he had been angry with her. Had he stopped loving her as well?

Hannah Schiltz arrived the next morning, and Kristoffer had scheduled his chores so that he was in the barn and could avoid her. Karoline had not readied Betsi. She told her nothing of the visit or its purpose. There was no benefit in Betsi worrying throughout the night for what was to come. Karoline had worried enough for both of them.

"Mrs. Olsen, would you make sure that Betsi is undressed from the waist down and put some extra sheets on the bed?"

Karoline went to Betsi's room and asked her to take off her pantaloons and lie on the bed. Not knowing why she was being told to complete these instructions, Betsi complied, but her eyes told

Karoline she was frightened.

"Betsi, that lady who came yesterday is not a midwife. Your father has decided that it is best for you if she removes the baby. She's going to help you this morning."

"I'm not going to have the baby? Jimmy and I aren't to be married?"

"Betsi, your father thinks this is for the best. This will be over quickly, and things will go back to normal."

Mrs. Schiltz walked into the room with authority. She set her case on the floor and removed several instruments. Pulling up a stool to the end of the bed, she asked Betsi to slide down to the bottom and lift her skirts. Karoline sat at her daughter's head and held her hand.

The woman used no morphine, no cocaine mixture, no chloroform. Betsi's screams reverberated throughout the house. Karoline felt helpless and tried to hold her down. These screams of panic and pain would be added to the catalogue of other gruesome sounds her children had made, sounds that Karoline played back in her nightmares.

"I think I am finished. She will bleed heavily for several days," Hannah Schiltz informed Karoline. "But you must watch her closely. If she contracts a fever, fetch Dr. Olsen right away. Don't call me. I don't go beyond today."

Betsi did not develop a fever, but her disposition changed. She grew lethargic and dour. She quit attending school and preferred to stay indoors. Her laugh and passion vanished, replaced by quiet and solitude. Karoline worried Betsi would never recover. Her body seemed to be mending, but her soul had been ripped out along with her child. Karoline could think of no medicine for it.

A month, then three, then six dragged by; yet Betsi resisted any attempts by the family to bring her back to normal life. She refused to help in the garden, she wouldn't come out of her room for violin concerts, and she pushed away her siblings when they wanted to spend time with her. Kristoffer complained to Karoline about her inability to "perk up" as he called it. On the farm, life and death occurred almost daily. To him, moving on instead of wallowing in loss healed all pain. Kristoffer accepted several months of her sadness, but by the sixth month, he was tired of her lack of motivation and believed that she had taken too much time to wallow.

On an overcast September morning, with the other children in school, Kristoffer sat Betsi down after their breakfast.

"It's time that you marry," he said. "You no longer go to school. You aren't taking your share of the chores. We don't know what else to do with you. I think if you had other worries, you would not drown in your sadness. I spoke to Lars Berg. He lost his wife in childbirth two years ago. He needs a wife to help him raise his five children. He wants to meet you."

"Lars Berg?" Karoline asked. "Isn't he in his thirties? Surely there is some other man closer to her age."

"Who will take her, knowing she is no longer pure? Young men want a fresh woman, not one who has been used by another man. She is not a widow. We have no dowry for her. She has no farmland. She is a loose woman who has been spoiled. Lars needs someone who will make a good mother and housekeeper. He knows her situation."

"I'm not marrying anyone," Betsi proclaimed. "And you can't make me." With that, she stomped off to her room.

Karoline said, "I don't disagree that she needs to marry. I have tried everything with her. She doesn't help out around the house anymore. She sulks and makes everyone unpleasant to each other. I think that Lars is too old for her, and five children are too many. She doesn't have the skills or the maturity to take care of them."

"I didn't say anything to you, but I have spent the last two months looking for a husband. Men closer to her age aren't ready to marry or they have already married. Only a man in a desperate situation would be willing to overlook her condition. He doesn't know about the child; he only knows that she is not pure. An older woman who would take on his children will come with children of her own. He cannot afford more mouths. Lars is a kind, moral man. He will be good to her."

Betsi married Lars Berg on October 8 in a small, private ceremony.

1905

Denison sat among the hills of western Iowa. Two crossed streets created the center of town. Main Street ran north to south along one of the largest hills. Broadway ran east to west on flat terrain. The middle of town, a cross between Broadway and Main, hosted a number of horses hooked to small, black buggies. Some buggies slogged through the loose dirt roads while others were tied up along the sides of the streets. A string of local businesses lined these two main streets, and merchants put their wares along the wooden sidewalks to tempt shoppers inside. A large brick post office sat on the north end of Main, and the modern three-story brick hotel was located just across the street.

Karoline, exhausted from her two-day journey from Jefferson, arrived in Denison late afternoon and found the hotel. She wanted some time to gather herself before she made the last day of her journey, so she registered for an overnight stay. She looked forward to a comfortable bed and a hot bath. She parked her wagon in a lot full of buggies and felt a twinge when she walked up the street and left Kristoffer behind.

Lodged in her room, Karoline stripped off her layers. Her skin, coated with days of dust, was burned and dry. She ran hot water into the bath, a luxury she had never experienced. The Denison Hotel, recently built, boasted of a large hot water heater for their patrons. With the tub full, Karoline slipped into the water and sat down, the water up to her neck. The luxury of being covered in water only happened when she went to the creek to swim, but the water was never this warm. She pulled out her hairpins and let her thick hair fall down into the water. Lying back in the warmth, Karoline closed her eyes and let her mind wander back to when she was a little girl in Norway. Her mother would treat her to a warm bath by heating water and pouring it into a large galvanized tub. Because her body was so small, she could sink down into the water as she was doing now. In her girlhood years, she liked to sit, imagining her adult life, until the water cooled. She pictured herself in Norway with a devoted husband and loving children. In her naïveté, she had only built a perfect image. Fate had not been a friend to her. Her life had been very far from ideal. She now wondered why she had been dealt such a difficult life. As a Christian, she believed that there was a purpose for everything. So far, she had not seen any purpose for a less than perfect husband or loss of her children or any of the other calamities that had befallen them. She prayed often and begged God to spare her some of her misery, yet He seemed to ignore her. There were years when she vacillated between belief and doubt. She believed her innocent Inger and Ole had gone to heaven, but she didn't know about Kristoffer. If her Christian faith was true, where would he end up?

Once out of the bath, Karoline used a brush to remove the dust and mud from her clothes. She wanted to drive into Soldier looking capable and solid. It was important to her that her community not see her as the poor widow who would need another man to take care of her. Karoline had no intention of remarrying. One man ruling her life had been enough.

Deciding to take a late afternoon stroll to see the town, Karoline redressed into her traveling clothes. She wanted to find the telegram office to tell her children she would be home late the next day so that they could set the funeral date. She knew that once again there wasn't much ice left in the wagon, and Kristoffer's body needed burying shortly after her return. The Soldier Lutheran Church's cemetery would be his final resting place. She left Tingvald in charge of securing a plot for him as well as for herself.

Karoline walked south along Main until she came to the crossroads and turned east onto Broadway. Many of the shops had closed for the day. She stopped at the druggist's to get directions to the telegram office. Curiously, it was part of the post office, which had already closed. Karoline would have to wait until morning to send word to Tingvald. The druggist recommended a café across the street and a little further east.

Koch's Café served German food. Denison's residents were mostly Irish and German. Without knowledge of another café, Karoline sat down, and making do with her poor English, ordered the schnitzel and sauerkraut. As soon as she put the sauerkraut in her mouth, she knew she had made a poor choice. The tangy, bitter flavor was very unlike her food. The schnitzel was well-prepared and filled her stomach well enough on its own. Most of the customers were speaking German, which made Karoline feel like the outsider she was. She felt her own loneliness without her family and community of other Norwegians.

This feeling reminded her of her years in Minnesota before she had met the other women. She missed those women, especially Lena, and wondered how they were and where they were. Karoline started to realize the number of friends she had made and left. Runa had sent her one letter since her return from Norway. Still unmarried and living on another farm, Runa had sent her condolences on Karoline's father's death. Both she and Runa had not lived the life they had imagined, but poor Runa had not advanced in life since Karoline's marriage. Karoline thought about Runa's future with no husband or children to take care of her in her old age. Would she die alone in a stranger's house?

Lena and Karoline had not kept in contact. Her last conversation with Lena had been about her task of getting to Norway. Thinking that she would not return, Karoline had made a proper goodbye to her friend. She missed Lena, who had been there for her in times of crisis. That generous woman had brought her through the worst time in her life, yet Karoline never knew of Lena's fate. Maybe she was still in St. Paul and had perhaps put flowers on Ingrid's grave a time or two? She was just the sort of friend who would look after the memory of a child not her own. Karoline hoped that Lena and her husband had bought their own farm, and maybe Lena had her own garden and house.

While she still saw Kristina on occasion, the women had been too busy raising their children and taking care of their houses to see each other very often. At first, they tried to commit to once a week. Eventually, it was every month when one of them would travel to the other's house for afternoon coffee. Now, if they saw each other four times a year, they were lucky. She didn't blame Kristina, but she wished the two of them had remained closer. She needed that friendship; she needed to share her triumphs and tragedies with someone who could see life from her perspective. She had wanted so badly to share Betsi's tragedy with her friend, but they had drifted too far apart to discuss something so shameful. When Betsi married Lars Berg, she had desperately needed to spill all of her dark feelings to another woman. Instead, Karoline pretended that it was a joyous occasion and put on a happy face. Karoline found herself alone in this new land, as alone as she'd been the first time she had stepped off the ship. Perhaps even more alone now that she didn't even have a husband.

The next morning, Karoline arrived at the post office to send her telegram as soon as it opened. She messaged Tingvald to set the funeral for two days from that day. A rejuvenating night of sleep, a clean body, and cleaner clothes had given her the boost to travel home that day. She left by ten in the morning. Karoline would arrive home late that day and looked forward to her own house and loving children.

When she went to the lot to retrieve her wagon, several vultures were on top of the covering. She shooed them away and started her final journey home.

1905

Karoline and Kristoffer sat with Tingvald in the parlor after supper. He had requested their presence, and Karoline knew that it probably had something to do with the young woman he had been courting. Now twenty years old, Tingvald had become a serious young man. His chest filled out with muscle, and he had grown a thin beard and mustache that matched his auburn hair. He did not, however, reach his father's height.

"Mama, *Fadir*," he began with a quavering voice, "I think it's time that I start to make my own money from the land. I've been helping in the fields since I was seven, and I haven't received one dollar from it. *Fadir*, you've always said that I was going to inherit part of this farm when I was old enough. You said that I could build my house on that land, get married, and raise a family like you've done. That time has come. Ella Evensen and I are planning to marry. I've asked her father for permission. He said when she's eighteen we can marry. That's in two years. In the meantime, I'm going to build a house. I need to make my own income to do that and save up for our life together. I think it's time to get my share of the land now."

Tingvald looked his father squarely in the eye the entire time. He kept his voice even and said his speech with as much confidence as any other man.

Karoline was so proud of her son. He had already gone to Ella's father. He was now coming to his own father. Just like Kristoffer, he was organizing his life and preparing for his future. Except she was sure that Tingvald had told Ella that he didn't have a house and hadn't saved any money. That would be the first difference between the two men.

"Tingvald, I did tell you those things," Kristoffer replied. "And I meant them. Someday you will inherit your portion of the land. It's too soon. Our family still needs the income, and I can't afford to give away a third of it now. Ingrid's husband, Stefan, has not asked me for any land. He is happy to receive his pay. What if I pay you what I pay him?"

Kristoffer had also kept his voice even and low. He kept his eyes directly on Tingvald's. Karoline could see an explosion coming. Kristoffer would never back down to his own son, and this was Tingvald's first time standing up to his father.

Karoline couldn't believe what he offered their son. Stefan did not receive much pay because he was also getting a portion of the land. Ingrid also had a big garden as well as chickens to feed them. Stefan had put his pay into raising hogs so that they would have meat to eat. Kristoffer was offering Tingvald much less than he would be paid as a hired man.

Tingvald leaned forward for emphasis. "Papa, that's not fair. Stefan's additional pay is land. Are you suggesting that as your son I have to work for my portion of the land as well? Do I have to buy it from you? If that's what you want, then I'll go work for someone else. At least then I'll receive a fair wage." Karoline could see Tingvald's eyes water, and his face was red. He stood with his hands balled into fists.

"Tingvald, you're getting out of hand. I haven't thought much about this. You have sprung this on me. Give me some time to think about it. I'm sure I can come up with something that will please us both."

Kristoffer's words seemed to calm Tingvald. He nodded his assent, let out his breath, and unclenched his fists. Karoline felt the tension in the room begin to dissipate.

In bed that night, Karoline brought up Tingvald's request. "What are you going to do about Tingvald and the land? You did tell him…"

Kristoffer cut her off sharply. "This isn't your affair. You need to stay out of this. This is between my son and me. I know what I said and I mean it, but it's complicated. We're not going to discuss this. Good night."

With those words, he turned over in bed with his back toward her to emphasize he was not to be bothered again.

In the morning, Tingvald and Kristoffer sat down at the table as they had every morning. Kristoffer talked about the day's work, and Tingvald occasionally looked over at his mother, who was frying doughnuts at the stove. He seemed to say, *Do you think he's going to give me some land?* She, in turn, looked back at him and gave a slight shrug.

Each morning, the men sat at the breakfast table and made their plans for the day. Each night, Kristoffer picked up a book and read after supper, and Tingvald went to the Evensens to visit Ella. Each day Karoline kept herself out of the conflict. The not-knowing went on for weeks.

During those weeks, the corn crops grew but would yield far less than other years. No rain fell when the corn was putting on its tassels. Kristoffer, always worried about money, decided that he would go north again. The corn wouldn't need harvesting until October, so he wanted to get in a couple of months of work before he needed to take care of his own fields. Several farmers up in northern Iowa raised large herds of cattle and always needed farmhands. Kristoffer no longer worked in the logging camps because it was a young man's job, a job that needed a strong body.

Tingvald, looking for an opportunity to make money, told Kristoffer that he too wanted to go north to work.

"Who's going to look after the farm while I'm gone if we both leave? I can't leave your mother without help, so you need to stay here."

"Why is it more important for you to make money than me?" Tingvald demanded.

"Because I have a family to feed, which includes you. You don't have a family, so you can stay."

Kristoffer turned around and walked away, his usual way to end an argument. Tingvald, standing in the middle of the yard, looked at his mother, who was standing in the doorway.

"Why does he always do that?" he asked. Why does he get to decide and then won't even discuss it with me?"

"Tingvald, this is your father's way. You know that. I'm not saying that I agree with it, but you should have anticipated his response."

"Mama, he hasn't even talked to me about the land. That was four weeks ago. He told me that he would have an answer. He's just putting me off."

"Let me talk to him after supper. For now, you'll stay here with me while he's north."

Knowing how much Kristoffer hated to be contradicted in front of anyone, including the children, Karoline waited until they were in bed to say something to him.

"Kristoffer, I don't think you're being fair to Tingvald. It's natural for him to want his own life, his own family. He's not going to have that if he can't make money working for someone else and he can't make money from the land."

"I told you not to get involved in this. If he's man enough to want his own life, then he should be man enough to confront me instead of sending his mama." With that, he turned over and didn't say another word.

After breakfast, Karoline went to the barn to speak to Tingvald while he was grooming the horses.

"You need to say something yourself to your father. I think I may have made it worse by speaking in your favor. He now thinks that you aren't man enough because you won't solve your own problems. He's leaving tomorrow. You can say something tonight or tomorrow morning. That way, he can think about it while he's up north."

What Karoline really meant was that Kristoffer could get his anger under control while he was gone. Once he calmed, he would be able to consider Tingvald's perspective.

While Kristoffer was saddling his horse and packing his supplies, Tingvald approached him.

"*Fadir*, you said you would give me an answer about the land, and I want that answer before you leave. If you aren't going to give me my portion and allow me to make my own money, then I won't be here when you return. I am going up to Sioux City to find work. Are you going to give me my share or not?"

Shocked, Karoline had never imagined that he would speak to his father in this way and threaten to leave him. She could see Kristoffer's face turning red and the vein sticking out on his forehead. There were very few times when she had seen him this angry.

"You ungrateful mutt! You didn't break the sod on this land! You didn't break your back every day to make this into a farm! You didn't build the house you sleep in! I did those things. And now, you think you deserve a third of it? What gives you the right? Real men go out and get their own land. They make it into their farm with their own hands. It was never given to them. They—*I* earned it! If you leave this farm, you're done. No inheritance. And you'll not show your face here again!"

Kristoffer stood—hands clenched, face red and quivering, neck muscles straining. Karoline could feel the breaking point. If Tingvald stood up to his father now, all would be lost.

"Stop it! Both of you, calm down. Kristoffer, you did tell him that you would give him a response, and he has respectfully waited for you. I've heard you tell all of the children how this farm will pass to the boys. It's time. You need to honor your words and give him the land…"

"Enough!" he screamed at her. He had turned from Tingvald to face her. "Enough, Karoline! I told you this isn't your business, yet you can't help yourself, can you? You had to step in and protect your son. That's the problem, isn't it? You've raised my sons to be spoiled like you."

"Spoiled? I work just as hard as you do. And my children are not spoiled."

"Yes, and you are too! You've been spoiled since the day I married you. You couldn't even get married in your *bunad*; you had to have a wedding dress like Queen Victoria. And you were too good to live in the dugout. You went running home to your parents when you didn't get your way, and I had to listen to all of the men in the camp tell me how you wore the pants. You also didn't last even two days in the field before you got the Svensens to feel sorry for you. You are more than happy to take charity if it means you get your own way. And you won't listen to me. You do whatever you please. I can imagine what the men in this town must say about me. 'There goes Mr. Karoline Olsen, the man who is run by his wife.' I can't even keep my head up in this town. My father told me not to marry you. He said that your family thought they were better than everyone else. The children in your family never worked for anyone else because they thought it beneath them. My father told me that you would not make a good wife because you didn't know what it was like to sacrifice. He said you were spoiled. And he was right. I'm tired of fighting with you. I'm tired of being married to you! I wish it had been you instead of Ole."

His last sentence hung in the air, frozen in time. The cruelty of it seemed to stop all other sounds: children, birds, even the sound of the wind. He continued to stare at her, and she could tell that he had meant the last sentence though perhaps not to say it aloud. The quiet stretched on until he finally mounted his horse and rode away from her.

1905

Leaving Denison brought Karoline both excitement and dread. She felt the anticipation of going home to a place where she belonged, yet she dreaded Kristoffer's funeral. Traveling from Denison to Soldier would take a full day, a day in which she would have to come to terms with her own feelings before she put herself on display.

This two-week journey had given her space to look at her own part in their marriage. It had always been easy to blame Kristoffer for every pain she had suffered. Karoline knew, though, that she had to take some of the blame as well. While Kristoffer was not the husband she had expected, Karoline was certain she was not the wife he had expected. Had she played the role of a wife who'd known her place, would he have loved her more? She was convinced that he would not have said many of the things that had caused her pain.

Traveling across Iowa and back had allowed Karoline's mind to travel back to the events that had built and torn down their relation-ship. In each event, she could see what role each of them had played. She wanted to make Kristoffer take all of the blame, but she had to be honest enough with herself to know that he should not be yoked with all of it.

His final words had been cruel. Yet, his characterization of her being spoiled and needing to get her own way had nagged at her throughout her trip. When she'd left him to go to Norway, her actions were far more extreme than necessary. She admitted that she could have moved into a boarding house in St. Paul or gone only as far as Chicago to make her point. However, she ached for her parents and used her daughter's death as an excuse to go home to them. As she thought back through each of her memories, she now could see how her choices were as much about her as they were about doing what was best for her children. She wanted to call herself a mother who was willing to sacrifice herself, but she knew that was not com-pletely true.

Many of her choices had been about herself. That beautiful white wedding dress had been an extravagance to show off. She could have been married in her *bunad* as all other Norwegian women had done before her. The years the Svensens had lived with them, Karoline couldn't even admit to herself that she loved the attention they'd given her until now. Being released from the fieldwork during Kristoffer's recovery had made her feel rescued again. If she had truly wanted, she could have continued to finish the plowing. She knew many farmwives who worked as hard as their husbands. He was right: she was spoiled.

Karoline switched from reflecting on herself to her daughters. What kind of wives were they? What kind of wives would they become? Did Ingrid ignore Stefan's wishes? Was she headstrong like her mother? She hoped that her daughter had a happy marriage. If she didn't, though, Ingrid would never say anything to her parents. She was not the type of person who spilled family secrets. Karoline doubted very much that Ingrid would ever show up on her doorstep with her bags packed and children in tow. And Betsi? She worried the most for this daughter. Since she'd left their house, she had had very little contact with the family. Would Betsi ever forgive them for what they had done to her? Did she carry the anger for her parents into her own marriage? How did she treat her husband? And how did he treat her?

Karoline's twin girls, Gunda and Sophie, were yet to be wives. Not only would they grow up fatherless, they would also no longer have an example of marriage, but perhaps that would end up being a blessing.

Karoline fervently wished that Kristoffer was alive so that she could apologize and admit she had been wrong. She wanted desperately to know if he still meant those awful words after he had calmed down. Did he regret what he'd said? Did he wish he could take it back?

Her last journey with him in his silent state had allowed her to reconsider their life together without interruption or re-direction. Most of their days had been spent in monotonous harmony, she thought. He had his daily routine, and she had hers. There were no cross words or conflicts. It was only when something stressful had come along that they seemed to show their worst sides. For her, she knew that she had reacted to his tone and actions. Her stubbornness never allowed her to give in. Somehow, she always got what she wanted or found another way to win. Thinking about Kristoffer's reactions, Karoline realized that he'd said things or made decisions out of fear: fear of losing control, fear of losing his reputation, fear of looking weak. Those last words he'd shouted at her were not about her; they were about him. "Mr. Karoline Olsen," she remembered.

Not understanding him had been her weakness in their marriage. As his mate, she should have seen through his commands to obey and understood that he needed to feel like he was the leader of his family. If she had realized this early in their marriage, she could have found ways to make him feel he was getting what he needed without giving up what was important to her. How could she have known him this long and not seen who he was?

The answer to that question was clear: she only thought of her own feelings and needs. She wished she could go back to the beginning, speak to young Karoline, and tell her that she must preserve his dignity at all costs. She was a smart girl. Certainly, she could have found a way to make him feel like she was obeying. If she could do that, then he would give her the kind of love she needed.

But she couldn't. He died believing he had married a horrible woman, one who had made his life miserable. While he was lying on a stranger's bed for five days, slowly dying, did he think about his life with her? Had he wanted her by his side? She had gotten no information when she was in Cedar Falls. There were no final words to replace the ones she heard: "I wish it had been you instead of Ole." Karoline's conflicted heart was still pained from every angry word Kristoffer had allowed to cross his lips, but she was also ashamed of her own behavior, her feelings vacillating so that she could neither completely hate him nor completely hate herself. She wished she could hate him and simply shut her feelings down, but her marriage had been too complicated for that.

1905

Sitting on a hill, overlooking the fields of dying corn, Karoline viewed Soldier Township. She could see her house, surrounded by those oak trees, and she was surprised that nothing looked different. Her house looked the same; the grove of trees looked the same. With such a major shift in her own life, she thought it odd the rest of the world had gone on unchanged. She took a deep breath and released it slowly, steeling herself for what was to come, and clucked her tongue to move her horses forward.

Pulling into their yard, Karoline was met by her children, who came running from various directions. Once they'd gotten to the wagon, they stopped and stared. No one spoke. Karoline could recognize the conflict of emotion on their small faces. Finally, Tingvald said, "We have the coffin in the barn. Is that where you want to prepare him? Or, do you want to take him into the house now, and we'll bring the coffin later?"

"I think we had better prepare him in the barn. I know it seems disrespectful, but there is a strong odor. I'm afraid it will permeate the house."

Tingvald jumped up onto the wagon seat and guided the bays to the barn where the men could unload his body. Karoline followed along to supervise the transfer. Tingvald and Stefan untied the tarp and began to roll it back. The smell of rot escaped from under it and assailed their noses. Both men and Karoline immediately covered the lower half of their faces with their arms and searched for cloth to make a mask. Their milk cows, frightened by the smell of death, bellowed loudly and moved restlessly in their stalls. Karoline walked out of the darkened barn and breathed deeply of the summer air. The men, faces now covered, climbed into the wagon to brush away the straw and bring down the wrapped body.

Looking at Kristoffer as they unwrapped him, Karoline suppressed her urge to gag. Aside from the horrific smell, she hardly recognized her own husband. The cartilage in his nose had decayed, sinking it into his face, and his skin had darkened from the decaying process. In an instant, she knew they could not have an open casket. She didn't think they could even have the service inside the house. Karoline considered having a private burial for their immediate family.

However, not allowing mourners to show their respect to him would be her last disrespectful act. Karoline's new understanding of how Kristoffer felt when he thought his reputation was being tarnished kept her from choosing a private burial. He would want people to be able to pay their respects. He himself had never missed a funeral.

"We're going to have a closed coffin. We will hold the wake outside. I know this is not the way things are done, but I think people will understand," Karoline said. Once she had made the decision, she stopped doubting herself and moved forward with plans.

The family held the wake in the grove of oak trees behind their house. Kristoffer was as solid as those trees, and Karoline thought he would like this new setting. They had carried all of their household chairs out to the grove, and she and the children sat in rows beside the coffin. Mourners trickled through, starting with Kristina. Karoline, who had been holding back her worries and feelings, felt a rush of emotions when she saw her friend. She did not have to pretend with Kristina. Her friend held her hand and sat next to her for several hours. There was no need to speak; each woman knew the other's thoughts. Karoline promised herself she would visit Kristina in the coming weeks and share the details of the final goodbye.

Each mourner stood at the casket for a few moments and then took their leave, giving Karoline a hug or a squeeze of her hand. Each one made sure to tell her how much they had admired Kristoffer or what a good man he was. Karoline's only response was "thank you" because she felt it was wrong to lie. She could not look them in the eyes and agree that he was a good man or that the community was losing one of their best. Some of the women surprised Karoline by telling her stories of how Kristoffer had shown up to help them plow their gardens or fix their stuck window or mend a broken axle on their buggy. Unbeknownst to her, Kristoffer had been there in other women's times of need. He had felt sorry for those who were husbandless. As women built the picture of this generous, empathetic man—someone Karoline didn't recognize—she began to feel irritated that he had treated other women better than his own wife.

One of the final mourners was Elfred Svensen. Elfred wore his best black suit with a white shirt. He was cleanly shaven and had carefully combed his hair back. Karoline usually did not see him so well-dressed. She supposed he had worn this particular outfit for Olof's funeral, but she had been too ill to attend it. Elfred sat behind her and said nothing, waiting for the last of the community members to leave.

The two of them finally alone, Elfred said, "I wanted to talk to you about Kristoffer. I know what happened the day he left; I'm sorry but Alex shared the details with me. I heard what he said."

"I'm so ashamed," she said. "My husband hated me and died with those last words still between us."

"Karoline, he didn't hate you. I know because he talked about you all the time. Besides, I lived in this house and could see how he looked at you. Kristoffer had a temper, and he was very impatient. I know he got angry with you, but he always felt bad afterward. Unfortunately, he never shared that with you. For some reason, he could never admit he was wrong when it came to you. I know he loved you very deeply. When you had smallpox, he was terrified you would die."

"But he said that he wished I had died instead of Ole. Those were his last words to me, and I know he meant them."

"He didn't mean them. I'm sure of it." Upon saying this, Elfred reached into his jacket pocket and pulled out an envelope. Karoline recognized the handwriting—it was Kristoffer's. As he held it out, she simply stared. "This came while you were gone. I checked the post office for your mail, and I pulled this out and saved it for your return. I wanted to give it to you myself."

Karoline finally took the envelope. Its contents would be one of two things: an apology or a request for a divorce. Once she read the letter, there would be no more from him. He would leave her with love or cruelty. She tucked the letter into the pocket of her skirt. She would decide later whether to read it or not.

Karoline invited Elfred into the house for a cup of coffee; she needed the company of someone who knew both of them well. The children volunteered to stay beside the casket through the night.

"Karoline, you should read Kristoffer's letter. I'm sure he wrote to apologize for his outburst."

"What if he didn't? What if he wrote to divorce me? Or to add onto the hurtful words he said to me? You weren't here. You didn't hear what he said or how he said it. I know he meant every syllable. If he was sorry, he would have taken them back, but he didn't. He mounted his horse and rode away. He told me I was spoiled. And I think he was right."

"Ha! *Ja*, he always said he married a woman who was better than he was. He was proud of that. He acted like he was irritated, but anyone listening to him could hear the pride in his voice. You were not some common woman who could butcher hogs or plow fields."

"He told me he was ashamed that I didn't stay out in the field when he was laid up."

"I'm sure he was just using that to hurl at you because he was angry. He was never angry that you couldn't work the fields. He was proud of you for trying even though he knew you wouldn't last. He didn't think you'd make the first day much less go out there again with your child in tow. He told Olof and me all about those days when he was in bed. His frustration got the best of him. I'll say one thing about him: he was a man with a temper. Most of the time, he kept it simmering. I'm not sure that was the best way, but it was his way. Once he was done being angry, he forgot all about whatever had set him off. Olof and I probably spent as much time with that man as you did."

"I don't know, Elfred. There was too much between us that you don't know. Maybe he was putting on a show for you? Never once did I feel like he was proud of me. Quite the opposite. I disappointed him in every way possible."

"I'm not sure you're right about that. I'll take my leave now. I hope you read the letter. I'm sure it will make you feel better. Kristoffer was a good man. And you are a good woman. I'll keep my eyes on you. You will let me know if you need my help, *ja*?"

"I will. Thank you, Elfred. You and Olof were such good friends."

Deciding she wanted to spend some time alone with her husband, Karoline left the house and returned to the grove, giving her children the rest of the night off. She told them she would keep the watch by herself. She settled a chair next to the casket.

"Kristoffer, I hope you can hear me. You didn't give me a chance to respond when you left, and this is the only way I can make amends. You were right: I am spoiled. As a child, I was always given whatever I wanted. When I became your wife, I took what I wanted. As much as I reminded you of your wedding vows, I had forgotten about my own: to love, honor, and obey. I tried to love you, but I gave up. I never even tried to honor you. And I think we both know how well I obeyed you. But I'm not going to take the entire blame. You had your faults as well. If you had given me just a little respect, I would have tried harder to respect you. I've thought about our marriage since the day I left to bring you home. You hurt me over and over. You treated me like a child who needed discipline. And like a naughty child, I pushed my limits and disobeyed you. We both failed. Now there is no way to make our marriage better. We are both left with bitterness. You wish I had died? Sometimes I wish I hadn't married you. Now the truth is out there for both of us."

After Karoline had spoken her true feelings, she felt released. Keeping her feelings pent up for years had only made her more miserable. Realizing it had probably been the same for him, she wondered why they hadn't shared them. She hadn't been raised in a silent household. Because he had said nothing, she had reciprocated. Fear of bringing more anger or another bout of silence kept her lips still. She had trodden gingerly in her own home to keep peace. Why? Had she ever really tried to have a quiet conversation with him about how he made her feel? She knew he didn't like conflict or to be questioned in front of others. That was his manhood he was protecting. But she had never known how he would have responded to a calm admission of feelings once the storm had passed. She could only blame herself for this one.

Karoline sat the rest of the night beside Kristoffer's coffin. Stress and the long journey assailed her will to stay awake. She dozed next to him, her head resting on her chest, dreaming they were back in Norway at Evensen Pond. Dangling their feet into the cool water, Kristoffer put his face close to hers and looking deeply into her blue eyes said, "I wish you had died." Karoline began to sob at his cruelty, and then she was suddenly holding Inger's dead body, which had rotted black with a sunken face. Karoline woke herself with her loud sobbing. It took her a moment to grasp where she was. His cruel words and her child's death—these events, she recognized, had been the most hurtful of her life. They even overpowered the best ones, like her first kiss at the pond. While she had been telling herself she understood her own part in their marriage's demise, Karoline knew she might never forgive him for all he had said and done.

If she didn't allow herself to forgive him, what would her life look like? Karoline would continue her years with this bitterness, allowing it to permeate every day, every week, every month, every year. It would make no difference to Kristoffer; she would be the only one of them to suffer from her inability to forgive. Her brain told her she needed to forgive him for herself. If she could, Karoline could then move forward in peace. However, Karoline could no more shrug it off than she could change her own eye color. It had become a part of her.

Kristoffer's funeral procession took place the next morning instead of after the usual three-day visitation. Since he had been dead for some time, there was no need for custom. It felt wrong to Karoline to break every burial tradition, but then Kristoffer's death away from his home was the ultimate change; the rest simply followed suit.

The family rose early to put on their best dark clothes. While Karoline was gone, Ingrid had remade one of Karoline's other tops so that she now had a black jacket to wear with her black skirt. She had also taken Karoline's wedding veil and dyed it black. The rest of the family had also refurbished or borrowed any necessary funeral attire. Her children and their families arrived at the house by ten in the morning to line up for the procession. Normally, the family and attendees would walk behind the coffin; however, the six miles to town made that rather difficult. Kristoffer would be buried in the Lutheran cemetery; they did not have a family plot. Karoline imagined Kristoffer's response to taking a parcel of their farmland to establish an Olsen cemetery.

The boys loaded the coffin into the back of their wagon, and Elfred brought his buggy for the women to follow behind. When they reached Soldier, the family lined up behind the wagon and began their walk to the church, adding mourners along the way, looking like two rows of black ants.

Reaching the cemetery, Karoline and the rest of the family stood next to the hole in the ground. Looking at the crisp sides of the hole, the spade marks visible, Karoline couldn't help but see the similarity to the walls of the dugout. Memories of her firstborn's death flashed through her mind, bringing back the pain and anger. While Kristoffer would lie next to his family throughout eternity, starting with Ole, Inger would lie by herself in an unknown place. Friends of Kristoffer stepped forward and lowered the coffin into the hole with ropes. The remainder of mourners fanned out around the gravesite within listening distance. Karoline shifted her view to the simple but well-built coffin, and imagined what he looked like inside it—she could only see his rotten corpse and not the one she had slept beside for twenty-two years. As Reverend Alden started the service, Karoline's mind focused on Kristoffer, her husband. She couldn't help but think that the condition of his body now matched his rotten heart, one that had been slowly souring from good to cruel since the day she'd married him.

Reverend Alden finished the service by talking about what a good man they were burying, a man who would be welcomed by the angels. Ingrid reached out for Karoline's hand and squeezed, sending her the message that she understood how hard it was for Karoline to listen to all of these false platitudes.

Tucked into Karoline's pocket sat the letter. After making and remaking her decision, she decided to throw the unopened letter into the grave so his last words would stay with his body. She was content she knew him well enough to know what they would say.

When the Reverend finished, the mourners said their own good-byes and drifted away from the gravesite, leaving Karoline and her family their space to say their own farewells. One by one, her children threw a flower from her garden into the hole, none of them shedding but a few tears. Finally, only Karoline remained. They instinctively knew she had her own words to say to him and gave her the privacy she desired. However, standing at the head of his grave, Karoline had no final words. She had said everything to him the night before. She reached into her pocket and pulled out the letter. As she held the letter over the hole, a hand reached out and took it from her.

"Karoline, don't," Elfred said from behind her. "Read the letter first and then I have something I want to say to you. Please. For me."

Karoline turned around and faced this long-time friend. "Only because you asked," she replied.

She took the letter from his outstretched hand, opened the envelope, and looked at the handwriting—a cramped longhand that was instantly recognizable. The letter was short in its content, and she read it quickly.

Karoline,

I want to apologize for what I said to you before I left, but you seem to know how to bring out the worst in me. I think that we have not been a good match. I thought if I married a Norwegian woman we would be compatible together. I realize now that it takes more than just the same language and place of birth to make a marriage, and I can no longer tolerate being with you. For that reason, I have decided to move out of our house and reside with Ingrid and her family. I will move as soon as I return from the north.

Kristoffer

How dare he? she thought. He could not tolerate her? Any remorse she had for her own part in their marriage was gone. Not wanting to spend another second being angry at a dead man, she threw the letter into the grave and turned her attention back to Elfred.

"What do you want to say to me?" She looked directly into Elfred's eyes.

"When the time is proper, I intend to ask for your hand in marriage. My brother and I have loved you since the day you first walked into your house and we had our stocking feet on your side table. We didn't want to sell our shares of the farm, but we agreed that it was the appropriate thing to do. If we had built our house just down from yours, one of us—probably Olof—would have eventually done something that would have gotten us killed. So, we moved to town, away from you, and watched you from afar, trying to look after you when we thought you needed it most. I truly think Olof died not from the pox but from the fact that he gave it to Ole and you. I know I'm laying a lot at your feet, but a good-looking woman with a farm will become a fair prize in this county. Before all of those men show up at your door, I thought I should tell you my intentions. I hope you forgive me for being so rude as to do it with your husband lying in his grave before us. I wanted you to read the letter so there would be no remaining words between the two of you. I hope you can forgive me."

Her mouth slightly ajar, Karoline replied, "I'm pregnant. I was planning to tell Kristoffer before he left, but everything got out of hand... Well, you know the story." She continued to watch Elfred, expecting him to make his apologies and walk away. A pregnant woman was the best deterrent for suitors.

"You know I love your children, Karoline. Like I said, I'll be back when the time is proper." With his final words, Elfred turned away from her to let her finish burying her husband.

"I guess I know what I'll name this baby if it's a boy." With a smile on her face, she turned around and walked back to her house.

EPILOGUE

Kristoffer had been married for two weeks when his father summoned him. Seeing the message, his stomach felt watery. He and Karoline started their married life living with her parents; they would be leaving for America in two days. Life at the Evensens' was drastically different from his home, and for once, he felt peace and comfort. There was no gloom or sulking or fighting. Mr. Evensen spoke in measured tones to his wife and children, which now included Kristoffer.

What could his father possibly want with him? Would he try talking him out of taking Karoline to America? Did he want to disparage him for staying with the Evensens instead of the Olsens? Whatever it was would be unpleasant to hear, but his sense of paternal duty prevented him from ignoring the command to visit.

When Kristoffer arrived at the farm, his father was outside feeding cattle, and when he saw Kristoffer, he indicated they would talk in the barn. Kristoffer noticed that the outside of the building was starting to show its age, the red paint faded from the sun. It would need a new coat soon, but he would not be around to do the work, which pleased him greatly. The inside smelled like hay and manure with very little light coming in due to its few windows. Kristoffer was familiar with the barn because he had often used it to escape his house when his father had gone into a rant or had hit his mother or one of the children. His father gestured to a discarded set of chairs from their kitchen and settled into one of them.

When Kristoffer heard his father clear his throat, a sound he made when he was about to say something uncomfortable, he knew this was not going to be a pleasant conversation. He thought it best to look down at his feet and listen, saying nothing in return so that the talk would end as soon as possible.

"I was watching you after the wedding ceremony, the way you hung onto that girl like you was a calf and she was your mother cow. You embarrassed me by acting that way."

When Kristoffer said nothing and didn't raise his eyes, his father took this as a sign that he should continue.

"I know you're in love right now and don't want to hear nothin' about your pretty little wife, but you need to learn a lesson before you learn it the hard way."

"I do love her," countered Kristoffer. At hearing the tone his father used when mentioning his "pretty little wife," Kristoffer couldn't help but stand up for her. "She loves me, too. She is already a wonderful wife and will make an excellent mother."

"Now you listen to me, boy. That gal is spoiled. Her parents have done for her so she's never had to do for herself. That dress she wore at the ceremony was shameful. Prancing around that church like she was Queen Victoria herself. Imagine her parents letting her wear a dress that was made for a queen. How much time and money do you suppose it cost them? That family spoils all their children. They've never had to work a day in their lives. How the hell do you think she's going to last in America? Just to survive will require both of you to work day and night."

"*Fadir*, she doesn't need to work. I'll work. She's been raised to do housework. Her mother taught her household skills. That's all we'll need."

"Boy, you don't know nothin'. It's going to take both of you out in those fields to scratch out a living. And she's not the right kind of woman for that work. But, you've gone and married her, so all you can do now is make the best of it."

"We will be fine. We'll both work hard and get our farm."

"You're not listening. You're dreaming and don't know the ways of the world. I'll say this plain. With her type of woman, you've got to put your foot on her neck. As spoiled as she is, she's going to question you and argue with you. No man tolerates that from his woman. You need to understand your duty as the head of the household. You make all of the decisions, and no one should question you. If your wife or child questions, give 'em a good slap. They won't question you again."

"*Fadir*, I can't hit Karoline."

"Then you aren't a man. You're a boy with a woman who runs him. You'll live the rest of your life hanging onto her skirt tails. You'll be the fool who is run by his wife. All the men will laugh behind your back and call you Mr. Karoline Olsen. No man worth his salt allows his woman to question him, tell him what to do, or disobey him."

"Karoline won't do that. I know she'll be the best wife a man could have. I've chosen well. I know it."

"Don't come cryin' to me like some woman when you've got problems. I won't feel a bit sorry for you. I'll say this once again, and then I'm done. You do what you want. If you want your wife to respect you and have respect from the community, then you've got to keep her in line. You can't appear weak like you were doin' at the church. You make your word law and don't never go back on what you decided even if you're wrong. She'll take advantage of that weakness and pretty soon you'll be changing your mind on everything. Don't allow her to make no decisions. Make her stick to her house. She'll get big bloomers and think she's your equal if you include her in your decision-making. I know you don't want to hear this, but if you give her a good beating every so often, she won't never forget who is boss."

Kristoffer's face showed his disgust at the thought of beating his beloved. He saw the sneer on his father's face and knew that his father thought he was weak.

"Humph. I can see this was a waste of my time. She's already got you wearing her apron. When you decide that you want her to respect you as a man, then maybe you'll listen to some of my advice. If she don't respect you, then she won't love you."

Kristoffer offered his hand as a man should do when saying goodbye. For the next two days, his father's advice rolled around in his head. As he watched Karoline, his father's words took away some of her shine. Kristoffer could see that she was spoiled. He had listened to her include her opinion when she spoke to her parents. She had definitely spent too much time and resources on her wedding dress, which was now packed away in their trunk for America. She would never wear it again until a daughter wore it for her wedding or until Karoline died and wore it to her grave. It had been a frivolity and a waste of money that they could have used toward their trip.

Kristoffer didn't want to admit any shortcomings about his new bride, but his father's accusations were not completely false. What if she didn't respect him? He had been bossed around by his father his entire life, and he had looked forward to having his own family and being able to have final say without someone questioning his decisions.

Until they were away from everyone, especially her family, he would not be able to determine what their relationship would be like, so his only option was to wait and see. He was certain, though, he would be able to have the kind of relationship with her that he thought appropriate, but he would never hit her.

CAROLINE OLSEN

AUTHOR'S NOTE

The Olsen family is my family. Caroline and Christopher Olsen came from Norway where we think they met, but they were married in America. Caroline came across with her sister.

Most of the book is fiction. My mother never knew her great-grandmother, Caroline, or her great-grandfather, Christopher. She knew a little of Caroline through family stories. She never heard anything about Christopher; therefore, his personality is from my imagination only. Most of the fictional children are named after their children, but their stories are also fictionalized. Some of their stories were created from other members of my mother's family. They were such good stories that I didn't want to leave them out.

Tingvald is my great-grandfather, and he was born on the ship going back to Norway. Caroline did leave Christopher for a year and a half when she became angry with him. Apparently, he was spending too much time with the Svensen brothers.

The idea to write this book came when I spent time with my mother, and she shared her genealogy book with me. She told me about Christopher dying and Caroline having to bring his body from Sioux City. My imagination took off, thinking about what must have gone through her mind on her way back to Soldier, Iowa.

Please read this book as purely fiction. I have no intentions of disparaging my ancestors.

On a historical note...

If you are Norwegian, it is difficult to trace your lineage because it was customary for a son to take his father's first name as his last name. Ole's son became Olsen. Each generation had a different last name. This practice stopped around the time the characters emigrated to the United States. All family members began to take the same last name as is custom today. I looked on several websites to get ideas for some of the surnames I used, and I found most of them spelled with *sen* rather than *son*.

The Norse language does not use the letter *c*. The name spellings in the book are accurate spellings. Kristoffer and Karoline's names were changed to Christopher and Caroline. In the cemetery, I found that Christopher's grave was spelled *Olsen*, but Tingvald's grave was spelled *Olson*. Why the name change in one generation is beyond me.

I decided that I wanted to retain as much flavor of the Norwegian tradition as I could; therefore, I decided to keep original spellings, both first and last.

Although he has been gone for some time, I am writing this to apologize to my grandfather, Glenn Olson, Tingvald's son. He was always very insistent that Olson is spelled with *son*; otherwise, people would mistake his family for Danish, God forbid.

Ann

Acknowledgements

I am extremely grateful to the people at Bookpress Publishing. Never in my wildest dreams did I think I would ever get my book published. Their support and encouragement have made this experience unforgettable.

I also need to thank the two women who gave freely (and I do mean free) of their time to help me edit this book. Kristin Jeschke—an excellent friend, teacher, and writer—gave me feedback while she was also giving feedback to her students. She made this book so much better. Jane Olson (not of my Olson family) offered her help in proofreading the book and read it multiple times to catch as many errors as she could.

My book club, The Big Read, were the first ones to read the book. They made me believe that it was good enough to put out there. Otherwise, it probably would have gone onto a thumb drive and stayed there for the rest of my life. Thank you for your support.

Thank you to John Kotz, my husband, for his continuous support. I didn't tell him I was writing the book until I was almost finished. He encouraged me, hauled my book boxes, went on research trips with me. He believed in me every step of the way.